THE GRAPE FARM

The Sequel to the *Berry-Picker House*
and *Lace Around the Moon*

By

Mary Pierre Quinn-Stanbro

NFB Publishing
Buffalo, NY

NFB
NFB Publishing/Amelia Press
119 Dorchester Road
Buffalo, New York 14213

For more information visit Nfbpublishing.com

Also By Mary Pierre Quinn-Stanbro

Fiction
Lace Around the Moon

Lace Around the Moon is a fictional novella, which is the prequel to *The Berry-Picker House*. It is the story of Jazz Singer Pierre's struggles to overcome the societal barriers that were rampant in New Orleans during the Birth of Jazz. It takes you through her life and shows how she not only persevered but came to find the one thing she had been searching for throughout most of her life. This story transcends you into a different time and place in history. You will want to experience all that the Crescent City has to offer… for all the senses!

Non-Fiction
The Bond of Blue

The Bond of Blue is a tribute to my father, Francis P. Quinn who was a Buffalo, New York Police Officer.

Dedication

This story is dedicated to my sisters (sissies) Kim Marie, Faith, Mary Grace (Gratia) and Kelly Siobhan. With sisterly love, all things are possible. You have taught me that and I am forever thankful for your love and support.

Ella Pierre Arnone, my goddaughter – Perhaps the next author in our family. You have a gift for writing.

SPECIAL THANKS TO:

Michael Marcklinger

Mary Ann Moriarity

Peggy Novara

Marie Schmidt

Erina Seaman Graham

Gene Stanbro

Doreen DeBoth – Designer – Cover and Back of Book

Julie Quinn Blyth - Editor

TABLE OF CONTENTS

Prologue	15
The Berry-Picker House Murder and Trial	17
Starting Afresh	35
The Grape Farm	47
Deeper than Skin-Deep	56
A Wonder of the World	63
Jazz Jam	70
Girl Talk	88
Affairs of the Heart	101
Forgive Me, Father, for I Have Sinned	112
Tonight's the Night	120
Taking Care of Business	126
Jewels	133
Secure Love	146
Rose Colored Glasses	151
Bienvenue – Welcome!	154
Exploration	159
Self-Actualization	166
Breaking Bread	170

Betrothment 179

Something Old, Something New … 189

Our Union Day 196

Irish Blessings 204

Hidden Secrets 209

Life Goes On 217

Moving Forward 223

Perseverance Hall 230

Amen 242

New Beginnings 249

Neutral Grounds 254

To Stop and Sense the Grapes 256

Epilogue 260

About the Author 262

PROLOGUE

Laissez les bons temps rouler!

Starting my stories with those words defines me in many ways. My name is Maria Pierre Quinones. However, I am known to my family, friends and even my adversaries as Pierre. I can say my name now without any apprehension or remorse, and most importantly with pride. I am a jazz singer from New Orleans, Louisiana (NOLA). When I was 14 years old, I gave birth to a son who I was forced to give up. By the grace of God, I recently found him and he is now part of my life. Along with that monumental experience, I also learned I have a granddaughter. With those new developments, I have come full circle. I am truly blessed.

I would like to share my story with you about reconnection, struggles and perseverance. We all have dealt with at least one of those issues at some point in our lives. Also, I believe anyone who may have been separated from loved ones for one reason or another will be able to relate to my life. Those feelings are shared in a verse from my song, "Lace Around the Moon." - "Whenever you look up and see the lace around the moon, know that our hearts will be together soon, with this, we will never be apart."

Everyone has a story to tell, but not everyone has the tenacity to share theirs...

THE BERRY-PICKER HOUSE MURDER AND TRIAL

While dessert of grape pie with vanilla ice cream was being served at the Naples Hotel in Naples, NY, a woman entered the room holding two babies. She walked over to Anna and Peter and gave each of them a swaddled infant. Anna came over to me, took me by the hand, and asked me to stand up as she put the child dressed in pink into my arms. Peter came over with the little one in blue. Anna said, "Pierre, there are some people we want to introduce you to. I would like you to meet little Phillip and little Pierre. She also introduced me to the woman who brought the babies as their nanny. Since the name I go by is Pierre, I longed to think that the little one in pink was my namesake. Anna saw the look of confusion on my face. She said, "I believe you knew that Peter and I tried for many years to have a child. We felt it wasn't going to happen for us. However, by the grace of God, we have been given these gifts of life. Pierre, you know how much I loved my twin brother Phillip.

Therefore, I wanted to name my son after him regardless of all that happened. I also felt it necessary to name my daughter after you. You are the epitome of what a strong woman is and I feel that with her having your name, that is what she will become."

It was such a feeling of joy holding baby Pierre and then baby Phillip. I just stood there in awe while a wave of happiness passed through my mind and body. Normally, I was not a person to show my emotions, but I couldn't help myself at that moment. My son Johnny, his wife Tee, my granddaughter Maria and my dear friend, newspaper reporter Greg Baynes, gathered around me when they saw I was tearing up. Maria said, "Gran Pierre are you okay? You don't seem to be steady on your feet." I assured them I was fine; just so elated to be experiencing the feelings I had flowing from my being. I said to Anna and Peter, "There are some things in your life that surprise you, take your breath away and leave you in a total state of euphoria. This is one of those times." Anna simply said, "It was meant to be Pierre!"

While sitting there at dinner with everyone talking and having a wonderful time, I found myself lost in thought. The past two days had been a whirlwind of activity. My mind quickly replayed the conversation I had the previous day while on the train from New Orleans, Louisiana to Naples, New York ...

Although Johnny and Tee read the articles Greg had written about me for the *New Orleans Observer* called, "The Perseverance of Pierre," I felt I needed to tell them the story in my own words. I explained to Johnny and Tee that when Storyville was coming to its end, I was singing at saloons and pleasure clubs both in the Quarter and in Storyville. Storyville was the red-light district of NOLA from 1897 to 1917. One evening, our band called the Lagniappe Orchestra, was finishing up our first set. We usually performed my signature song "Lace Around the Moon," at that point in our show. A very young man approached me. He had been paying enough attention to know that I would welcome a whiskey - neat. Politely, he asked if he could talk to me about my music and the song, "Lace Around the Moon." He said the words spoke right to his heart. The young man shook my hand, introduced himself as Phillip Wilcox and told me that he was from a small town called Naples, in the Finger Lakes region of Central New York. It wasn't the proper time for us to get into a long discussion as I had to get ready for my next set. So, he asked me if he could pay me for my time in discussing what jazz music was all about and how I was living it. I was quite taken aback by him and his proposal. However, with the substantial amount of money he was offering, I found I couldn't resist. Since I didn't know him,

I told him my bandmate Jeremy would also need to join us. He was fine with that.

We met Phillip a day or two later in front of Mahogany Hall and took him all over Storyville and into different pleasure clubs where the real jazz was being played and lived. We had a wonderful time. He was so appreciative and genuinely interested in what I had to say. We stayed out quite late and by the end of the evening, we were all exhausted. Before we parted ways, I extended my hand for a farewell handshake. I was startled when he boldly kissed my hand. No one had done that since Timothy C. Anderson (TCA) many years ago. He then placed my hand on his heart and much to my surprise, he repeated the words to my song, "Whenever you look up and see the lace around the moon, know that our hearts will be together soon." I was so overcome with emotions by this gesture that I took off my precious strands of glass beads that I always wore, which were a gift from TCA, and gave them to him as a parting gift. Phillip told me that after he returned home, he would be heading off to law school. We didn't make arrangements to write to each other after our brief time together, but not long thereafter, his letters started to come to me. We developed a friendship through letter writing over the next 16 years. I sometimes thought of him as a son and confidant. Although we were living in two different worlds, hundreds of miles apart, we were connected through "Lace Around the Moon," and what the song meant.

About 17 years after first meeting Phillip, I received a telegram from Anna, his twin sister. In the message, she asked if I could please come to Naples and be there to support her and Phillip. She didn't go into all the specifics, but she said they both desperately needed me. Anna said she would pay for my transportation there. Since I was no longer singing in the clubs regularly, I did have the time to go. However, I wasn't sure it was something I wanted to do at that point in my life, but her message spoke to my heart. The next day, I sent a telegram back to Anna and told her I would be in Naples within a week.

When I arrived, Anna picked me up at the train station. While driving to her family home, she started to cry. I put my arm around her and said, "Child just take a breath. Let's pull over to the side of the road so you can collect yourself and tell me everything that happened."

She explained that Phillip had fallen in love with a young girl named Carmelita who was one of the berry-pickers staying at the berry-picker house. Phillip learned from Carmelita that she was staying in Atlanta, NY with her aunts, uncles and cousins for the harvesting season when she wasn't at the Wilcox farm. However, she was born in New York City and lived there most of the year with two of her aunts. That was all he really knew about her and nothing else mattered to him except that he loved her.

Although Phillip was old enough to be Carmelita's father, that didn't stop him from pursuing a physical relationship with her. Unfortunately, Carmelita allowed the torrid affair to happen; she was an eager participant at first. At the same time the two-year affair took place, Phillip was still married to a woman named Florence, who was Peter's sister.

During the third year of Phillip's and Carmelita's relationship, Phillip found out Carmelita was pregnant and he assumed it was his child. However, she told him that it was not his; it was her young lover Ritchie's baby. Ritchie was also a berry-picker who worked at the Wilcox farm. Phillip lost his mind and in a fit of rage, he took a shovel and killed her with it. They arrested Phillip for Carmelita's murder and he was put in jail to await his trial.

To be of help to Anna and Phillip, I spent the next few months leading up to the trial at the main house on the Wilcox property. Every day, I would go and spend time with Phillip, sitting outside of his cell, I became his confessor and Phillip became mine. I told him things that I never told anyone about my life in NOLA. But the one thing I never could tell him was that I had a son. Unfortunately, I learned things about Phillip I wished I had not, but we were connected. I felt that I was in the right place during that turbulent time. Although I was in turmoil over the entire situation, I knew I had to be strong for Phillip and for Anna. But at the same time, my heart ached for the family of Carmelita and for Ritchie, who lost his love.

The court proceeding started and was over quite quickly. It was hard for all of those involved in this tragic situation to fathom what came out at the trial. Turns out that many years prior to Phillip meeting Carmelita, he had relations with a young woman named Angela Caprizzi. Everyone called her GG and she worked as a berry-picker at the Wilcox farm. Their relationship never evolved since Phillip's main focus was going to law school. Both of them went on with their lives and Phillip never thought of her again. That was, until the trial.

On the opening day of court, all hell broke loose. The district attorney called a woman named Kay Fletcher to take the stand. Kay explained that many years ago, she worked at the Wilcox farm as a berry-picker and would stay at the berry-picker house for many harvests. She went on to reveal that about 19 years ago, her best friend Angela Caprizzi (GG) confided in her that she had gotten pregnant by Phillip Wilcox and she was moving to New York City to have the baby. Kay later learned that she had a baby girl and named her Carmelita! The entire courtroom was in an uproar and the judge had no other recourse than to adjourn for the day.

The following morning, everyone in the courtroom including Ritchie learned that the baby boy Carmelita had been carrying was most likely Phillip's, not Ritchie's! This information came from the coroner who was on the stand testifying that he used blood analysis to come to his conclusion. When Ritchie heard this, he lost his mind and killed Phillip by stabbing him in the back with his trimming shears that he used to cut grapes off the vines while working at the Wilcox farm. When that all happened, I was in shock. It was like I was watching a silent movie unfold right before my eyes. Three lives were lost because of hidden secrets and deceptions – oh what a tangled web.

In Phillip's defense, he never knew that GG was pregnant. However, his parents did. They gave GG a large amount of money to take care of her baby as long as she never told anyone that Phillip was the father, not even Phillip. They thought if he had the responsibility of a child, he wouldn't be able to pursue his law degree and have a wonderful life. What they did was out of love and they thought they were doing him a service. Oh, but what a disservice it turned out to be. They set in motion the tragedy that unfolded. Phillip murdered Carmelita, who was his daughter. Even more tragic is that when he took Carmelita's life, he also took his own son's life.

The hardest part of the entire ordeal for me was when Anna and I had Phillip's burial down by the tree, the same tree on the Wilcox property where Phillip had taken Carmelita's lifeless body and was holding her when the police arrived. I learned that Phillip had given the beads I gave him, which were a gift from TCA, to his precious Carmelita. She was holding them when Phillip killed her and they fell and broke on the floor of the berry-picker house. It turns out that Anna had picked those beads up after the murder. I was astounded when she took my beads out of her pocketbook and placed them on Phillip's casket at the end of the very brief ceremony. It was a feeling of closure for me. I was letting go of my past and all the sadness of Phillip's death and the entire ordeal that had taken place over the past few months. My focus began to shift to returning home to NOLA.

A few days later, before heading to the train station, I went to the berry-picker house. In a trance-like state, I took a pencil out of my pocketbook and left a message on the wall of the berry-picker house. The same wall that previous berry-pickers had signed over the years while they were staying there during the harvesting seasons. The same wall that GG and Kay Fletcher had signed many years ago. I knew Phillip was gone and would never be able to read my little message, but I left it there all the same. "Phillip, many years ago, I had a son I chose to give up. When I met you, it was somewhat like meeting my own son. Over the years and through our letters, you became the son that I never had the pleasure of knowing. I will hold you close to my heart."

After I left my message, my eyes looked over all the other names and writings on the wall. I remembered seeing a little note in the right-hand corner down toward the bottom of the wall that read, "Forgive me, Father, for I have sinned." I had a feeling it was Phillip who wrote it and I thought someday I would try to uncover the story that might go with the message. It was very intriguing to me.

It wasn't until I heard Maria ask if she could have another piece of grape pie to take back to her room that I came back to the present time. She had finished her first piece in two minutes and said it was the best dessert she ever had!

The meal we all shared was delicious. However, I was getting very tired and needed a whiskey – neat, upstairs in my room. It had been a long train ride from New Orleans and sharing my story with Johnny and Tee about the berry-picker house murder and trial left me exhausted and drained.

Before calling it a night, Peter proposed a toast, "To Miss Pierre, Johnny, Tee, Maria and Greg. Thank you for all coming from so far away. We are honored to have you here with us. *Laissez les bons temps rouler* – let the good times roll! The one request that Anna and I would like to make of your time in Naples would be to have you all agree to perform at a small jazz music event at the Naples Hotel on your last afternoon here with us." Peter said that the local people were intrigued with me and even considered me to be a celebrity. Since my song, "Lace Around the Moon" had gained national notoriety, he and Anna thought if I would be willing to sing a few of my songs, with the accompaniment of Johnny and Tee, it might be a way to heal some of the wounds that were still open.

Since it had been quite some time since I had performed on stage, I was ready and wanted to quickly agree. However, I first wanted to make sure that Johnny and Tee would be willing to accompany me with a set of songs. They brought a smile to my face when they both enthusiastically said, "*Laissez les bons temps rouler!*" Maria even said she would also like to sing some of the songs. Since Johnny, Tee and I already had a set of songs that we used in New Orleans when we would perform together, it wouldn't take too much practice to make it happen. Anna said there was a piano in the front bar area of the hotel that Johnny could use for the event. She already cleared that with John and Kelly Arno, the proprietors of the Naples Hotel. They would have it placed in the area where we were having dinner, as it could hold about 150 people if some of the tables were taken out. Anna and Peter thanked us for our willingness to do this for them.

Peter then took Johnny, Tee, Maria and Greg to the front bar to have a look at the piano to see if it needed to be tuned. I was getting excited about this opportunity to perform for the people of Naples.

While I was settling the bill, Anna told me that she needed to mend fences with her close-knit, small community of Naples. The village had been through so much with all that happened with Phillip's murder of Carmelita. Many people realized that Anna had nothing to do with it, but since she was his twin sister, some still held resentment towards her. She thanked me profusely for agreeing to have a jazz afternoon at the end of our stay. Anna felt it would be a small way for her to give back.

Since no one else was around us, Anna discretely asked me who TCA was. I physically felt a sharp pain in my heart when she said those words. She explained that earlier in the day when she picked us up from the train station, I dozed off in her automobile and she heard me mumbling, "TCA, TCA." The only thing I could think of to say to Anna at that moment was, "He was my former employer, mentor and lover who never physically loved me." I told Anna I would tell her more about him when I could.

Anna, Peter and their babies were tired from the day's activities. I knew they would want to be getting their children down for the night. Peter said they would be heading back to the grape farm for the evening. Although they did not have their permanent residence there, they had a few rooms in the main house where they would stay from time to time when they didn't want to travel back to their main home in Geneva, NY, about 30 minutes away.

While wrapping up the night's festivities, Anna and Peter wanted to know if there was anything we would like to do while we were in Naples. Johnny leaned over to me and asked if it would be possible for all of us to go to Niagara Falls. He said he had always wanted to experience visiting one of the wonders of the world and since he speculated it was only about three hours away, perhaps it could happen. I responded, "We would love it if we could take a trip to Niagara Falls. Although we realize it might take up an entire day, the experience would be something we would be grateful for." Peter and Anna had a quick conversation and Anna said, "Peter will not be able to join us. However, I would be delighted to make a day of it with all of you. We'll get on the road early and I will pack a picnic lunch we can eat there. How would the day before the jazz event be for our outing?" After seeing the look of excitement on everyone's face, I told Anna that would be fantastic! Anna then asked if we would mind if Gene, her farm manager and part owner of her grape farm, came on the trip with us so he could drive one of the automobiles. I told her that we wouldn't mind at all!

We all left the restaurant area and went to the hotel lobby. It was there we said goodbye to Anna, Peter and Charles Watkins, their friend and family attorney who had also joined us for dinner. A young couple was standing nearby who looked like they wanted to say something but were hesitant to approach us. Anna recognized them and asked them if she could help them with something. The young girl wanted to know if the woman in the green dress was Miss Pierre. I approached her and told her that I was indeed Pierre. She said her name was Ella and her brother's name was Noah. They had learned from their parents, John and Kelly Arno, the owners of the hotel, that I was going to be staying there. She unexpectedly blurted out, "We love you Miss Pierre and are fans of yours!" I would expect those types of encounters back in New Orleans but not in Naples! Ella explained that she read the "Perseverance of Pierre" articles that were in the *Naples Newspaper*. The encounter left me somewhat shocked but I remembered Anna told me that there were articles in their newspaper after the Berry-Picker House Murder Trial about my connection with Phillip. However, I didn't realize the articles Greg had written about me for the *New Orleans Observer* were also being published in Naples!

I thanked Ella and Noah for their kind words. We chatted for a few minutes and they told me their parents were also teachers at the Naples High School, in addition to owning the Naples Hotel. Anna chimed in and invited them to the jazz event the following Saturday afternoon at the hotel. Anna said that we needed a name for our event. Maria spoke up and said, "Let's call it our "Jazz Jam!" Anna said she absolutely loved that idea. She told Maria that back when she was a girl about her age, she would come to the Naples Hotel for dances her parents would host. At those dances, they would sell jam, juices, pies; things they could put their berries and grapes into. Anna then told Maria, "You are onto something young lady – I think we will sell some grape pies at the Jazz Jam! I'll ask our local pie lady in town, Marjorie, and see if she could have about 50 grape pies prepared by then. The proceeds from the sale of the pies will go to Carmelita's family."

Before Anna left, she suggested she would come by the following morning to pick us up and take us to Grimes Glen, a park in Naples with historic waterfalls. When we were finished there, she said she would like to have us head over to the grape farm for a light lunch with grape pie for dessert. She thought Greg, Johnny, Tee and Maria would like to walk around the property and maybe pick some grapes. We told her that sounded wonderful. However, we asked her to make it later in the morning; we needed to catch up on our sleep.

Anna also said that the following day she was going to have a couple of automobiles dropped off for us to use for the week we were there. The vehicles belonged to Peter's electrical engineering business. We all just looked at each other and laughed at her generous offer but explained that none of us knew how to drive an automobile except for Greg. Since we were able to get anywhere we needed to go in NOLA by walking or from lifts from friends, there was no need for an auto. I was surprised when Greg said, "Just one vehicle will be necessary. I can now add chauffeur to my list of credentials!"

Once upstairs at the hotel, Johnny, Tee and Maria kissed me good night and headed to their adjoining room. Greg had his own room, paid for by the *New Orleans Observer*, since it was a business trip for him. While in Naples, he would be writing follow-up articles to the original ones he had written about me.

Greg said he would love to have a nightcap. I wasn't even surprised when he pulled out his brown paper bag with whiskey in it. We raised our glasses and Greg said, "To you Pierre and all you have accomplished since finding out Johnny was your son!" We didn't talk much and just finished our drinks. He reached for my hand, kissed it and said good night.

I went to sleep that night in my comfortable hotel bed but not before replaying the events of the past several days in my mind. I thanked the Lord when sleep came upon me without any dreams I could recall.

The next morning, I woke up earlier than I expected and went to look out the window of my room which faced Main Street. I thought back to when I had previously been in Naples and had traveled down the very same road on my numerous visits to see Phillip in jail while he was waiting for his trial to begin.

Reflecting upon when I first met Phillip and the journey that began after that initial meeting, brought me to tears. My mind began to replay all those events that changed my life. I suppose it was only natural that I kept thinking of Phillip. But I also started to think about TCA after Anna told me I said his name in my sleep. It is funny how the mind works. Sometimes it just won't let things go. Other times, it protects you by not letting things stay.

I got my thoughts and emotions in check after that journey down memory lane. My clothes were still in my suitcase so I picked out the outfit that was the least wrinkled and did myself up for the day. Having the opportunity to spend quality time with my newly found family and friends thrilled me to my core. I was looking forward to starting the day and my new life.

STARTING AFRESH

When I heard my people chatting and their footsteps, I went to them and suggested that we get some coffee from downstairs. It was a beautiful sunny day so we decided to take a walk down Main Street. Johnny, Tee, Maria and Greg were surprised by how small, clean and quiet Main Street was. None of them had ever been to a small town before. This was all new and fresh to them and they embraced the simple experience. It was a wonderful first morning for all of us! However, there was quite a bit of difference in terms of the weather between the two cities. In New Orleans in the fall, it was still in the 80s at times. We were not accustomed to the weather in Naples where it was in the 50s! Needless to say, I would be asking Anna if there was a shop nearby where I could purchase everyone a jacket. I never thought about it before, but it could be possible that colder weather makes a person's blood thicker to help keep them warm. And with us from the South, our blood needs to be thinner to keep it from boiling and causing us to overheat.

After our walk, we went back to the hotel to get ready for our outing. True to her word, Anna pulled up in her vehicle and had another man with her who was driving a 1930 Cadillac V16. Greg was quite impressed with the auto! Back in New Orleans, he drove an older model Tin Lizzie that had seen better days. It was the vehicle he was assigned for his job as a reporter with the *New Orleans Observer*. His eyes lit up when he was handed the keys. My eyes also lit up when Anna gave each of us a jacket and did a good job of figuring out our sizes. She explained that Peter's electrical engineering company had their employees wear jackets with the company name Ellis on them for advertisement and warmth.

Eagerly, we put on our jackets and Johnny, Tee and Maria got into Greg's borrowed vehicle. I got into Anna's auto and Greg followed us over to the Glen. Once there, we walked to three different waterfalls that were absolutely beautiful. The entire area was a Naples landmark. We spent about an hour there admiring the picturesque scenery. After that, we were ready for some relaxation. Anna said there was a lunch prepared for us back at the grape farm. Greg was again excited to be able to take my people back to the farm in his beautiful ride. Anna asked him to follow us. Since we had some time together, I started to open up to Anna about TCA. I told her about how he orchestrated my professional singing career.

However, I still was not comfortable to say much more about my personal relationship with him.

When our two vehicles pulled up to the Wilcox grape farm, Gene the farm manager, was waiting outside. He was a pleasant-looking man with beautiful blue eyes that seemed to look right into my soul. We followed him and Anna into the living room of the main house so we could put our bags down. Maria was excited to go outside and look around so we walked down into the vineyard. We were surprised to see quite a few people working in the fields. Anna explained that since it was harvesting season, the Mennonite workers were there for a couple of days at a time to pick the berries and grapes. Since Maria had never heard the word Mennonite before, she decided to call them men-in-tights! We couldn't help but laugh at her little joke. Maria reveled in the new experiences she was having since arriving in Naples, especially learning all she could about grape pies!

From there, we walked over to the berry-picker house. As far as we knew, Maria wasn't aware of what happened there, with the murder of Carmelita and we didn't think it was appropriate to tell her, at least not at that time. We all went inside and Maria said she thought the berry-picker house was so small and cute. She started to call it the "little house" and eagerly went room to room marveling at how neat and orderly it was. Anna explained that the house was built around the turn of the century. The inside was framed in oak and the outside was made of pine. It was approximately forty feet long by twenty feet wide with four rooms. Anna had Maria come into the front room to sign the wall and leave a short message in the section that had been set aside for visitors. Maria couldn't believe she was allowed to write on the wall along with her parents!

After Tee and Maria left to go to the main house with Anna, I felt it necessary to show Johnny where I had signed the wall when I was at the grape farm after Phillip's murder trial and death. He read what I had written, "Phillip, many years ago I had a son that I chose to give up. When I met you, it was somewhat like meeting my own son. Over the years and through our letters, you became the son I never had the pleasure of meeting. I will hold your memory close in my heart. Just as you had taken my hand to your heart back in New Orleans so many years ago – it is when you take another's hand to your heart, forever now, we'll never part." Johnny started to cry when he read my words. I too was crying. I held him tight and we embraced for a few seconds. He looked at me and took my hand and placed it on his heart. He said, "Mother we will never part again." We both composed ourselves and walked hand in hand up to the house.

Gene prepared a lunch of grilled cheese sandwiches and tomato soup for us. Maria's eyes lit up when she saw that there were two grape pies set off to the side. She told her parents she didn't even want lunch, just the pies. Tee told her she would first have to have a sandwich before she could dive into the pie.

When we were done with lunch, Anna explained that she and Peter had a formal event that night that they needed to attend. She said she would drop me off at the hotel and Greg could follow with Johnny, Tee and Maria. To be honest, we were glad to have the rest of the afternoon to ourselves. Anna packed up the rest of one of the pies for us to take back to the hotel. She thought we might want to spend the next day at the grape farm again, learning how to cut grapes off of the vine and prep them for a pie. Maria enthusiastically blurted out that she would love to do that! Anna also suggested we go for a long walk down to the tree at the end of their property. The tree was said to have mystical powers. Johnny, Tee, Maria and I said we would enjoy that very much. Gene was rather quiet during lunch. However, he said he would like to make us a special supper the following evening if we were up for it. I looked at my people and didn't even need to respond for them. They all blurted out "Yes, yes please!"

Greg said that he would love to join us the following evening for dinner. However, over the next several days, he would need to focus and work on his articles for the *New Orleans Observer*. He said that he was going over to the newspaper office to meet with the reporter who was assigned to collaborate with him on the articles they would be publishing.

Since Anna wanted Greg to be able to use the borrowed vehicle for work, she asked us if 1:00 pm would be a good time for her to pick us up the following day. We looked at each other and I spoke for the group with a definitive "Yes, that would be great. We could have the morning to get ourselves together and have lunch before being picked up."

We thanked Anna and Gene for the delightful lunch

and told her it worked out well that she and Peter had plans for the evening. I explained that Johnny, Tee, Maria and myself were anxious to start putting my song "Christmas Dishes" to music. Although we only had the guitar Tee brought with her to use, we at least wanted to get our harmonizing, music cords and notes figured out.

Anna dropped me off at the hotel and gave me a very endearing hug. She said she appreciated me sharing some information on TCA with her earlier in the day and looked forward to future conversations if and when I was up for doing so. Standing outside of her auto, Anna said, "I feel you do trust me as a friend and confidant. I want you to know how much I appreciate and respect you. I love you, Pierre." It came from my heart when I replied, "I love you too, Anna, and am very comfortable with you. Therefore, I feel I can ask you to tell me a bit about Gene." She explained that with her living in Geneva and now with the twins, she couldn't devote the needed time to the grape farm so she searched for someone to go into a business partnership with. Anna said, "I heard about him from other farm owners in Naples and Canandaigua and he came highly recommended. He definitely knew his farming and management. After we had several meetings and discussions to go over the finances involved, Gene bought into the farm and he has been running the day-to-day operations. It turned out to be a great business deal for both of us. Peter and I trust him and have developed a strong friendship with him. Gene is a good man and somewhat of a diamond in the rough – he just needs some polishing."

Greg dropped off my people and headed over to the newspaper office. We had a productive afternoon working on "Christmas Dishes" and didn't realize how much time had gone by until Greg came in and said, "I am hungry. Anyone else care to join me for supper at a little diner I saw down the street?" We all eagerly said – "Yes!" I remembered thinking that Greg seemed to be in a particularly good mood. He definitely had a skip in his step and a smile on his face.

After our meal, Johnny and Tee had Maria turn in early for the night. Maria gladly agreed to go to bed in the room she was sharing with her family. Her only request before going to sleep was to have a piece of grape pie. Since she arrived in Naples, that had become her favorite food item! We all had a piece of the pie that Anna had packed up for us earlier in the day. Maria's day was then complete and she kissed us goodnight.

I had Greg, Johnny and Tee join me in my room. Earlier in the day we were able to purchase two bottles of whiskey from the bar. They also generously provided us with four glasses. Although Greg and I liked our whiskey - neat, Johnny and Tee preferred it on the rocks. The four of us sat around the little table that was off to the side of the room and brought over chairs so we could all be sitting around the table as I started to unfold my story to them. Up to that point, I never had the opportunity to tell Johnny my story, from my lips. Greg shared background information with Johnny on how he came to be my son when he first found out he indeed was. However, he didn't tell him everything, especially who his father was. I felt it was the time for me to share parts of my life with him, if he wanted to hear it.

Greg poured us all a drink and as I had done before, I closed my eyes and the words from my heart just started to flow…

At 13 years old I became pregnant. It wasn't under the conditions I would have liked it to have been, however, that didn't matter to me.   When my stepfather found out, he sent me to the Ursuline Convent in New Orleans to give birth to you, Johnny. Sister Veronica, the head nun, and the others at the convent were very good to me while I was there.

After you were born, I remember holding you in my arms and singing to you for the first few days of your life, when I was allowed to nurse you. From that moment on, I never wanted to be separated from you. However, I was told you would have to be given up for adoption. That broke my heart and body. I had already bonded and connected with you. Sister Veronica said I would be going back to Mississippi, where I was originally from after I healed from childbirth. I believe it was divine intervention when those circumstances changed as Sister Veronica ensured that I never went back to Mississippi.

I found myself unable to continue with my telling my story. The words just stopped. My tears were flowing and I was sobbing. It was just too raw and emotional for me. Johnny saw the difficulties I was having and came over and sat next to me. He looked me in the eyes and said, "Mother, I have been blessed to meet and marry Tee. But when my own daughter Maria came into my life, I realized that was the most precious bond two human beings can share. You must understand, for all of my life before I met you, I wondered where you were and why I wasn't with you. Sometimes at night, I would cry myself to sleep just hoping and praying that whoever my mother was, she loved me. I never had the same feelings about finding my father. That didn't matter much to me. So, I do not need to know who he is or was. You are both my mother and father; you are all I need. When I first met you many years ago when Ms. Flordie brought me to you for piano and singing lessons, I grew to love you then. I even wished you were my mother. How miraculous it was that my wish came true! All those years when you were my musical mentor, you were actually my mother. It doesn't matter how I came to be yours. My life is now complete knowing that I am and going forward, let's start afresh."

Johnny's words comforted me to the point I was able to tell him that if he ever changed his mind and needed to know more about who his father was or even if he wanted to know more about my life, I would tell him. But for the time being, I was glad the tumultuous subject did not need further discussion. Every family has it hard, this was just our hard. But what was remarkable to me was that all my hard was before I had my family and now that I had them, all of my struggles were soft in comparison.

We sat there for a few minutes in silence. Each of us had our own thoughts running through our minds. It was then I realized I needed more time at the grape farm. I told the others I would be staying on a bit longer. I also said I would let Maria know about this new development in the morning. To my surprise, they thought that would be a very good idea. They realized I had some issues to resolve in Naples and perhaps new friendships to cultivate.

We finished up our drinks and called it a night. Greg said he would see us the following evening at the grape farm for dinner. I walked him to the door and let him know how much I appreciated him being there with us; he fit in with our pack.

I went to sleep that night in peace.

THE GRAPE FARM

The following afternoon, it was actually Peter who picked us up at the hotel. He explained that Anna had been at the grape farm all morning getting things ready for us. We pulled into the driveway and I thought to myself, next to Saint Louis Cathedral and Jackson Square in New Orleans, the grape farm was becoming my favorite place to spend time.

We had a fantastic afternoon. Gene took us into the vineyard and gave us all a set of trimming shears along with a quick lesson on how to hold the grapes and use the shears to clip them at the right point for efficient release from the vine. We spent about two hours out in the vineyard with the other berry-pickers and "men-in-tights" working on our task and bonding. It was such a simple time but one I would cherish forever. I was with my people and friends, just taking in the intoxicating smell of the grapes. We were in grape heaven and our hands and clothes proved that. Anna came down two hours later and suggested we all go to the main house and clean up.

While we were doing that, Gene went and got his tractor out of the barn and put the grape trailer with benches on to the back of it so instead of walking down to the tree, he would drive us. We didn't refuse his gesture and walked over to the barn where he was waiting for us. Gene placed a little step at the back of the trailer to assist us in getting into it. I felt a flicker of excitement when he took me by my hand and helped me get seated on the bench.

Gene stopped a couple of times for us to get off and walk around the different areas of the vineyard. At one of those stops, Maria let out a scream. Johnny asked her what was wrong. She said there was a monster with spikes coming out of its head over in the row of grapes. It was then we saw a large deer running away from us. Gene explained it wasn't a monster but a 6-point buck who was hungry and liked to eat the grapes. Gene's words calmed Maria down. "The big buck likes grapes as much as you Maria! He just doesn't have his in pie." We all laughed at Gene's light-hearted comment and he continued to drive us down to the tree. As we came out of the thick brush, we were amazed at how large it was!

Gene helped us off of the trailer and we walked over to the enormous oak tree. He said that people would hold hands and make a human circle around it. So, we all held hands. I was surprised when Gene asked me if he could hold my right hand. Johnny held my left hand. The five of us circled the trunk of the tree and Gene said, "Everyone can say a prayer of thankfulness for this special day together." We all bowed our heads for a moment of silence. After we let go of hands, I said, "Amen!" Maria asked if she could walk over towards the water. Johnny and Tee went with her. Gene and I sat on a little bench under the tree. We didn't say much to each other but just sat there looking at my people over by the water. Gene broke the silence when he said, "It is the simple times like these that are the best. Miss Pierre, you and your beautiful family are warming my heart." I started to reply when Maria came running to us and asked if we could go back. She wanted to eat more grapes!

We headed back to the property going through the heavily wooded area. When we came into the clearing it was a   picturesque sight. Rows and rows of grapes glistening in the sunlight. I could smell the aromatic scent of the grapes. As we approached various parts of the vineyard, he explained the different types of grapes that were full and heavy on their vines. The different areas included varieties such as Worden, Sheridan and many sections of Concord. Those grapes were dark red or purple in color. There was also a smaller group of green grapes that Gene said were Dutchess.

Since it was getting late and everyone was hungry, Gene said he would drop us off at the barn. I enjoyed the entire trailer ride through the vineyard and I particularly liked when Gene again took my hand to help me off of the trailer. His hands were so strong and I felt a pang of sadness when our hand-holding ended. We all walked over to Anna and Peter who were waiting for us at the house.   Gene said he needed to put his tractor away and get dinner ready for us. They had us enter through the front door into the living room where there was a beautiful display of cheeses and wine. The wine glasses were extraordinary. Anna explained they were her parents and she only used them for special occasions. There was even a glass for Maria filled with homemade grape juice she and Gene made. She asked us if we would prefer white or red. After all the wines were poured, Peter made a toast to our good health. He said he and Anna wanted the night to be special for all of us. His parents were watching their babies back at their home in Geneva, therefore, they would be able to stay late without worrying about little Pierre and Phillip.

I couldn't help but notice the smells wafting over to us from the kitchen. They were intoxicating. I recognized the familiar scents of New Orleans, however, I also got a whiff of a hearty type of meat I couldn't recognize. It tantalized my taste buds. I didn't want to be rude and ask what the delicious smell was so I just sat there taking in all the different aromas and the wine that was dancing on my tongue. Wine was never my drink of choice, but what I was drinking was very pleasing.

While we were relaxing, there was a knock at the front door. Peter went and opened it for Greg. He seemed to be in a very good mood. Peter offered him a glass of wine and he sat down next to Johnny. The two of them were having a private conversation and both of them were laughing at times. They really seemed to be bonding. It made me happy to see my son having a good time with Greg, my second son.

After 30 minutes, Gene entered the room. It was so strange to me that I did a double take. I had always seen him with a cap and overalls on. But now he was dressed in a collared white shirt and clean dungarees. He wasn't wearing a cap. Instead, his hair was neatly combed. Up to that point, I didn't even know he had hair! He was an attractive man. I couldn't believe that thought just went through my mind. Gene said, "Could I take the liberty of seeing you to your seat in the kitchen, Miss Pierre?" He reached for my hand and with his other hand he placed it in the small of my back and helped me to my feet. We walked into the kitchen with him still holding my hand and he seated me at the head of the table. Anna and Peter followed with Johnny, Tee, Maria and Greg.

The table was beautifully set. There was a white linen tablecloth, napkins and a dish at each place setting. They did not all match but that did not detract from the intent that was evident in the time taken to put this together for us. I commented to Anna how lovely everything looked and I asked her what were the unusual flowers on the table. Anna said, "I cannot take any credit for the supper that has been prepared. Gene is responsible for this entire feast! And let me tell you the man can cook." Gene explained that the flowers on the table were called hollyhocks. They grew wild in the area and come in blue, pink, purple, red, white, yellow and even black.

Johnny asked Gene what the aromas were. He said he could make out the red beans and rice but there was a distinct smell he couldn't put his nose on. Gene explained that he wanted to make a meal for us by incorporating New Orleans and Naples staples. Deer meat is a popular dish in the Finger Lakes region as they are abundant. Gene thought a deer roast would be a nice accompaniment. My people and I were not accustomed to deer meat but it all smelled appealing. We all chimed in that we would love to try it. I don't know what the man did to make the dish taste so wonderful, but wonderful it was. And how he knew to prepare the red beans and rice just as we had back in NOLA was quite impressive.

There were also a couple more bottles of white and red wine on the table. Gene told us that he made his own wine. I couldn't help but think he was a very versatile man. Not only could he manage a grape farm, set a table, prepare a meal and make his own wine, he was also humming "Lace Around the Moon." I began to think that Gene may have gone to all this trouble to please me and I liked that thought. I was very flattered.

After dinner, Gene asked all of us to go into the living room so he could clear the table and set out the desserts. I asked him if he would like some company while performing the chores. He said, "That would be great." I explained to Gene that I was the queen of dishwashing. He looked at me with great appreciation when I uttered those words. He said that whiskey goes great with dishwashing. He poured me a glass and I dove into my chore. I never enjoyed washing dishes with someone as much as I did that evening with Gene. We just chatted about the meal and his wine. Even when I was in Naples a few months ago, I didn't partake in any wine drinking. However, the wine that Gene had made and served was so smooth going down. I told him I preferred his red wine to his white. He explained that with the dishes he prepared, the red wine was a better accompaniment. However, he wanted us all to have the opportunity to try both. He was definitely a thinking man.

We finished our grape and apple pie desserts and chatted a bit more. However, Anna could see we were fading. She said she and Peter would drop me off at the hotel and asked Greg if he would take Johnny, Tee and Maria back there.

Gene helped me up from the table and he, Anna and Peter walked all of us out to the autos. Anna asked me what we would like to do the following day. All of my people said that they would love to sleep in! They were not used to eating so well and often and it took a lot out of them. Also, Johnny said they would like to take the day to prepare for the Jazz Jam that was only two days away. Greg again explained that he would be working all day at the *Naples Newspaper*. No one else saw that Anna winked at me and said to Greg, "You certainly do take your professional responsibilities seriously! I admire your strong work ethic!"

Greg suggested we could all meet up at the Naples

Hotel the following evening for our last meal there. Since we would be going to Niagara Falls the day after that, it would be our last opportunity to dine together. I told Greg I liked that idea very much and we could call it our "Last Supper." It was sad but true it might be quite some time before we would all be together again in the same way. Also, the realization my people would be leaving in four days was heart-wrenching. Anna and Peter said a last supper would be really nice and they would love to join us! Greg added he may be bringing a reporter from the *Naples Newspaper* with him. He said that person would like to meet us. This time it was I who winked at Anna and said to Greg, "We will all look forward to meeting the reporter you have been so diligently working with!

After arriving back at the hotel, we all looked at each other in the lobby and decided to turn in early. I went to my room and got ready for bed. Having a nightcap did not even sound appealing. I was tired and just wanted to shut my eyes. Sleep came quickly and I didn't get out of bed until 10 am! After waking up, I recalled that I dreamt of Gene. Perhaps it was because of the stir I felt when he took my hand to help me onto the trailer. I couldn't remember any of the specifics of my dream. However, Gene was obviously on my mind.

DEEPER THAN SKIN-DEEP

I didn't hear any of my people stirring until 10:30 am. Maria knocked on my door and came in. She looked refreshed and was raring to go. She said she wasn't even hungry. That in itself was surprising. But she was anxious to start rehearsing for our event in two days. She was so excited to be part of our first family performance. I told her that I was also excited. Maria and I sat down and had our first grandmother/granddaughter conversation. I learned that she loved music and someday wanted to be a singer just like her mother and me. She loved her parents very much but sometimes felt lonely. Although she understood that her parents had to work hard to keep a roof over their heads, she still wished they were not gone so often.

I asked how she liked school and how her grades were. She said school was easy for her and she consistently received grades in the 90s. But then Maria stopped talking. I looked at her and again asked her if she liked school. I felt terrible when Maria started to cry. She said that until recently, she didn't like school. However, when her classmates learned she was my granddaughter, things got better. I told Maria she would need to fill me in on what exactly she was talking about. She took a deep breath and said, "Some of the mean children at school said I must have been adopted. They even go so far as to say, "Hi yellow Maria." I didn't even know what that meant until I asked Daddy. He explained that some light-complected black people were called "high yellow." My daddy and you are black and my mama is light-skinned black. Why do I have even lighter skin with some freckles and reddish hair? If I didn't get my complexion and hair color from you and my daddy's side, I guess it had to be from my mama. Gran Pierre, why are some people so hurtful?"

I told Maria I couldn't explain exactly why people are the way they are. It is just human nature that some are good and kind while others are not. As to why you are so fair-skinned, I will leave you with this thought, "It doesn't matter the color of your skin. What matters is that you are loved by your daddy, mama and me. You have been created through the intermingling of all of our genes. Our blood is running through you and it is red. Red is the most powerful color of all. And every human being's blood inside their body is red, no matter what color their skin is on the outside. We are all the same under our overcoating."

Maria calmed down a bit and gave me a big hug. She asked if we could keep our conversation just between the two of us. I promised her I would. She didn't need to know why I made her that promise. But it was for a good reason, and one I intended for her to never find out about, at least not from me. I didn't want her or her mother to know that I had recently been given information as to who Tee's father may have been. It was only speculation, but it would explain Maria's fair skin, freckles and reddish hair. Perhaps some Irish blood was also part of Tee and Maria's undercoating.

There was a knock on the door. It was Tee. She asked Maria to get ready for our practice session. Tee said she hoped Maria wasn't talking my ear off. I told her that couldn't be possible and winked at Maria as the two of them went to their room. It was then I decided that after I returned to NOLA, I would be visiting Maria's school. I couldn't make things all better for Maria with her issues of ethnicity. However, I could do something positive with the children at her school that would bring them all together with music. Music does not segregate, only people do that.

About 30 minutes later, we all went downstairs for brunch. We needed some nourishment before we started our vocal workout. After we finished eating, we spent the next three hours going over our set. I knew we sounded good. That confidence comes from years of practicing and performing. We were ready for our performance the day after next.

Johnny, Tee, Maria and I went back to our respective rooms. We needed to get ready and dress for our dinner later that evening. I didn't know if Gene would also be joining us, but I hoped he would be. Instead of wearing one of the green dresses TCA bought for me, I decided to wear a form-fitting black one I brought. My body had a sturdy frame and curves in the right places. I was what some people referred to as "thick." And in the black dress I would be wearing, I was hoping there would be one certain person there who preferred thick to thin.

Johnny, Tee and Maria came over to get me so we could all go downstairs to the dining room together. My people all cleaned up nicely! I may have been overdressed for the occasion, however, Tee said to me, "Pierre you are alluring in that dress! Anyone who doesn't think so must be short-sighted. I hope that nice man Gene will be joining us this evening, as I believe he would love to see you in it. He seems to fancy you." There it was! I had confirmation that someone other than myself thought that he may be taking a shine to me. It made me feel good and shiny.

We entered the dining area and I saw Greg with a very striking blond woman sitting at a large table. Anna, Peter and Gene were also seated there. When Greg saw us enter, he jumped up and escorted us over to the table. He was beaming. He said, "Everyone, I would like you all to meet Miss Michele Grands. She is the reporter from the *Naples Newspaper* I have been working with on my "Perseverance of Pierre" articles." It made me happy that Greg had also taken a shine to someone and it was the lovely lady he just introduced to us. She was the reason for Greg's zealousness to go to work at the *Naples Newspaper* and why he had been wearing a smile for the past few days.

Gene got up from his seat and asked if I would like to sit next to him. I accepted his offer and he pulled out the chair for me. He told me he took the liberty of bringing some of his wine to the hotel for our dinner since I told him how much I enjoyed it. The waiter came over and poured us all some wine and Maria was given grape juice that Gene had also brought. It was surprising to me when Greg asked everyone to raise their glass for a toast. He said, "I am so appreciative to be part of this evening. I consider you all to be my new friends. We may live several hundred miles apart, but to quote a phrase of a great singer I know from New Orleans, "Whenever you look up and see the lace around the moon, know that our hearts will be together soon." We all said cheers and I told Greg he did a great job on his toast!

The meal that evening was lovely. The conversations were light and comfortable. It was a group of people from Naples and New Orleans who found common items to discuss and share. No one seemed to care what each other's ethnicities were. I couldn't have asked for more at that point in my life. However, I was saddened when I thought about my people going back to NOLA. It hurt to think of being separated from them. But I told myself I would be going back home in a couple of weeks. It wasn't like I would never see them again. Unfortunately, I always seemed to be getting ahead of myself and not taking the time to live in the moment and enjoy what I had. I decided not to reflect on their upcoming departure but to enjoy the next few days with them. That gave me some peace of mind.

We didn't want to stay out late since we would be getting up early in the morning for our trip to Niagara Falls. Everyone said goodnight to each other and I made a point of telling Michele how much I enjoyed meeting her and I was looking forward to the article she was writing about me. We briefly chatted about her job with the *Naples Newspaper*. She shared with me that she was very appreciative to have the job of a reporter considering it was unusual for a woman to hold that position. However, the owner of the newspaper was a forward-thinking woman named Destiny Swarovski. She encouraged other women to break barriers in the male-dominated industry, just as she had done, and she hired her right out of college. Michele said, "I want you to know Miss Pierre, I admire you and marvel at your accomplishments as well." She shook my hand and winked when she said, "Strong women have to stick together." I, in turn, hugged her and told her I hoped to see her at the Jazz Jam. Greg overheard our conversation and brazenly said, "I too hope Michele will come to the Jazz Jam, with me!"

A WONDER OF THE WORLD

Early the next morning, Gene and Anna pulled up to the hotel. He jumped out of the auto and ran over to get the door for me. Anna said she would prefer to sit in the back seat. Since it was going to be a three-hour ride, she could use the time to take care of business paperwork. I looked forward to being seated next to Gene for the long ride to Niagara Falls.

Greg, Johnny, Maria and Tee followed in Greg's borrowed ride. It was a beautiful autumn day and I enjoyed looking at all the farms we passed along the way. Gene told me that farming was always in his blood. He grew up on a farm in New York State, where his father was also a farm manager. However, it wasn't until later in life that he came back to farming. He was born in a small town three hours outside of New York City called Norwich. When he was a young man, he moved to Buffalo, NY for a job in Communications. That was his livelihood for over 30 years. When he retired, moving out to the country was where his heart took him. For the next several years, he worked on different farms around Canandaigua Lake where he gained the necessary experience needed to one day own a farm. Fortunately, he heard through friends that Anna was looking for a farm manager and business partner. Gene said, "Since I have been part owner and the manager of the farm, my vocation has been very rewarding. I believe that things happen for a reason; it was meant to be that I came to the Wilcox grape farm."

Anna was so quiet in the back seat I forgot she was even there. That was until she interjected that going into business with Gene was the best decision she made for the grape farm!

Gene and I continued to make small talk. There were not any uncomfortable lulls in the conversation. I was genuinely interested to hear about his life and let him do most of the talking. I was still too guarded about my own and just not comfortable opening up to a man I barely knew about all I had been through. At least not yet.

The time flew and after two hours, Gene said we were approaching Buffalo, NY, which was sometimes referred to as the Queen City. He explained it was the largest and most prosperous city along the Great Lakes from the end of the 1800s right up until the beginning of the 1900s.

We were still about 45 minutes from our destination. Gene thought we would all like to stretch our legs for a bit and have a refreshment. He heard of a new restaurant called Cole's that was located in a former Pierce Arrow showroom and suggested we stop there. He signaled to Greg who was behind us to pull over so he could tell him of our brief side trip.

Within 15 minutes, we pulled up to the restaurant on Elmwood Avenue. Upon entering, there was a very long bar off to the side adorned with gigantic chandeliers. The floor was done in black and white checkered tile. The establishment definitely had a NOLA feel to it. The host showed us to our table and we explained we would just be having drinks. However, that changed when Maria said she was hungry so we also ordered some french-fried potatoes. After we finished our refreshments, we paid our bill and used the facilities. We were then our way and excited to reach Niagara Falls.

Gene and I picked up our conversation where we left off. He said, "I have gone on for hours telling you all about me. Would you tell me a little something about yourself Miss Pierre, that I don't already know from reading the "Perseverance of Pierre" articles?" I thought to myself for a minute before responding to him. I didn't want to get into any of my deep, dark secrets so I kept my response light. I said, "I have never seen snow or tasted it and that is something I have always wanted to experience." I was surprised and intrigued when Gene said, "Well we are going to have to make that happen.

You will have to come back here in the winter and I would like to be there to see you when you first look up to the winter sky and taste the falling snowflakes." I told him that was a lovely thought and that maybe it would one day happen. Gene was becoming someone I wanted to get to know and experience small things like snow tasting with, so I asked him to please, just call me Pierre. For the third time in my life, my frozen heart was melting. Perhaps the third time could be a charm.

Greg brought along his work camera on our outing. When we arrived at the American side of Niagara Falls, we got out of our vehicles. Maria ran over to the railing and was jumping up and down with excitement. She said she had never seen anything so lovely or heard anything so loud in her life! We could hear the roar of the Falls and were mesmerized by their breathtaking beauty. Gene explained we were at the American Falls, which is the second largest of the three waterfalls that collectively are known as Niagara Falls.

Greg took a picture of all of us in our new Ellis Electrical Engineering jackets while we were up against the railing overlooking the Falls. Oh, what a sight we were! Greg promised to get us a copy of the picture he took. He said it would be a great photo to add to the article he was writing for the *New Orleans Observer* and for Michele to use in the article she was working on for the *Naples Newspaper*.

After we spent about 15 minutes admiring this majestic wonder, Maria asked if we could dive into the picnic baskets Anna had in her vehicle. That young lady certainly did love food! Anna laughed and asked Johnny and Greg if they would bring the baskets over to a table in the park area. We all partook in the scrumptious sandwiches and other treats that Anna had packed for us.

After we finished our picnic meal, we went back over to the Falls for one last look. I said a silent prayer of gratitude. I had so much to be thankful for since finding Johnny and my new family and friends. We started to walk back to where we had parked our autos. I was taken by surprise when Johnny hugged and kissed me and said, "Mother, I consider you to be one of the wonders of the world."

We headed back to Naples. After driving for about three hours, we were back at the hotel. Gene and Anna dropped me off. He helped me out of the auto and up to the door. I felt like a schoolgirl out on her first date. He gave me a little kiss on my cheek and said to have a good evening. Spending the day with Gene made me look forward to spending even more time with him.

Greg dropped off the others and said he had to get over to the newspaper so he could write his story about our day's events and develop the photos. Since it was still relatively early, we thought a stroll down Main Street might do us a world of good. We needed some physical activity after having been in the auto for so many hours. Although we were not hungry for a meal, we picked up some cheese and fruit from the little delicatessen that was not far from the hotel. A leisurely night in with some of the wine that Gene had given us with a cheese spread would be perfect. Then it was early to bed so we were refreshed for our Jazz Jam the following afternoon.

JAZZ JAM

I woke up early the next morning. Although I was still tired from our trip to Niagara Falls the day before, I just couldn't sleep in. Excitement and anticipation were flowing through my body. The night before, I laid out one of the beautiful green dresses TCA bought for me many years ago, as I had decided I would wear it for the Jazz Jam. For the first time in a long time, it didn't sadden me to think of him. It was going to be a wonderful day, I just felt it.

Fortunately, Johnny and Tee brought nice outfits with them from home. However, I was worried that Maria might not have dress-up clothes to wear. I looked through some of the other dresses I had packed and there was one in my belongings that would do. Even if it was loose on Maria, I had a belt she could use that would bring it in.

Noises were coming from my adjoining room. My people were also up early. I knocked on their door and asked Johnny and Tee if they would like some coffee. Both in unison said, "Yes please."

Since the event wasn't starting until 1:00 pm, we had plenty of time to get ready. I had Maria try on my dress with the belt. It was a bit large on her but she looked lovely. We had a leisurely light breakfast of grape scones and fruit. I told Johnny I was going to go see if Greg would like some coffee. He said not to bother; Greg had stopped in their room and told him he had to go to the *Naples Newspaper* office. However, he would be back in plenty of time for the event. He also told Johnny that he would be picking Michele up and bringing her.

After finishing breakfast, dressed in casual clothes, we went downstairs to have one last practice session before our show. The staff members greeted us as if we were celebrities. To them, I suppose we were. They asked us if there was anything we needed. We explained we were just going to go over our set and hoped we wouldn't be in the way. They said we were of no bother as they already had the room all set up. The manager, Terry came into the room and introduced herself. She told us she was Gene's sister and was delighted to meet us. The entire staff couldn't have been more accommodating!

When we walked into the back room, we couldn't believe what they had done! There were gold, green and purple beads hanging from the chandeliers. They moved the tables to the back of the room and had chairs set at each table so people could have a place to put their drinks and grape and berry pies. With the room being configured that way, there was plenty of space for Johnny, Tee, Maria and I to stand in front of the room with the piano. There were elegant flower arrangements on each of the tables that were adorned with purple tablecloths. They thought of everything!

We practiced for about an hour and were pleased with how we sounded. When we were finished, we went back to our rooms to relax for a bit before we had to get dressed. Shortly thereafter, there was a knock on my door. Anna was standing there with a shimmering purple dress and black fancy shoes in her arms. She said she thought Maria might like to wear the dress. It amazed me how she had an uncanny knack for anticipating my needs. She also brought a bouquet of hollyhocks. She knew I liked to wear a flower in my hair updo and she thought Tee and Maria would also like to cut a few off to wear in their hair.

Johnny was getting dressed in their room. Tee, Maria and I did the same in my room. Tee looked spectacular in her golden dress. She had a lovely figure and her outfit complemented her curves. She wore her hair down with a hollyhock placed off to one side. What took my breath away was when Maria walked out of the side room. I shed a few tears when I saw her standing there in the dress and shoes that Anna brought for her. Tee had done her hair in an updo, just like mine, and placed a hollyhock in her hair. She looked stunning! I told Tee and Maria they were gorgeous. Maria said, "Now is your time to show us how you look in your dress." After dressing, I walked out and Tee whistled. They both told me I looked beautiful in my green dress and I felt beautiful. Without even planning it, we were all dressed in the colors of NOLA – *Laissez les temps bons rouler*!

The three of us walked into Johnny's room. My boy looked so dapper in his crisp white shirt, black pants, golden vest and a tie with the same NOLA colors. My people swelled my heart with pride. We walked downstairs to the lobby. Noah and Ella, the proprietors' children were there and rushed over to us. Ella took Maria's hand and asked her if she would sit with her after the performance. I was glad to see a friendship developing. They were relatively close in age and seemed to enjoy each other's company. What I also saw was young Noah looking at Maria with a little gleam in his eyes!

Promptly at 1:00 pm, Peter and Anna escorted us to the front of the room. The applause seemed to go on for at least a minute. Peter had to ask everyone to please take their seats and get ready for the show. The Arnos then walked up and took center stage and thanked everyone for coming out to the Jazz Jam. They explained that all proceeds raised from the sales of the pies, and a portion of the drink revenue would be donated to the family of

Carmelita. She didn't even need to explain who Carmelita was to the group; they all knew.

Anna took the time to tell the crowd how much she appreciated the turnout for the event. The room was packed. All the seats at the tables were filled and people were lined up against the walls. Anna then said, "I want to introduce you to Miss Pierre, her son Johnny, his wife Tee and their daughter Maria from New Orleans, Louisiana, otherwise known as the Crescent City. Without further ado – let the good times roll!

We sang our hearts out for the next 45 minutes! Back in New Orleans, we would end our first set with "Lace Around the Moon." However, for the Jazz Jam, that was our first song. This brought the audience into our fold right from the beginning. Based on the applause we received, it was a very good decision. We continued performing popular New Orleans tunes for almost the entire set. However, what the audience didn't know was that we had a special treat for them at the end of our show.

Tee, Maria and I joined hands and presented "Christmas Dishes" a cappella. I sang the standard verses and Tee and Maria sang the chorus. In the middle of the piece, Johnny performed a short bridge on the piano!

Christmas Dishes -

Another year around the holiday table,
she looks around and thanks God she is still able
to use her Christmas dishes for yet another season.
Perhaps at times it has been for selfish reasons.

To her they simply mean so much
and with her extra loving touch,
she softly lays them gently down.
Longing to have family and friends all around.

With these Christmas dishes,
all she wishes
is for another year with them all.
Life hasn't been easy, but she still moves forward
standing strong, standing tall.

With these Christmas dishes,
she also wishes for relief from her pain.
Since having lost loved ones, makes it hard for
happiness to remain.

But the love she has for her family and friends will be
what keeps her going through the years,
until the years end.

Sometimes there may be one less place to set,
but she tries to think of that without regret,
knowing that the same plate may have been used by
ones missing,
is her Christmas gift – thoughts of reminiscing.

The food is not all that matters
but that they have chosen to gather.
The meal is what unifies,
but these Christmas dishes are the bond that ties.

With these Christmas dishes,
all she wishes
is for another year with them all.
Life hasn't been easy, but she still moves forward
standing strong, standing tall.

With these Christmas dishes,
she also wishes for relief from her pain,
Since having lost loved ones, makes it hard for
happiness to remain.

But the love she has for her family and friends will be
what keeps her going through the years,
until the years end.

These dishes are a blessing that she loves to share.
Using them is her way of showing that she cares.
Thoughts of her children one day using them lightens
her soul,
so keeping them with family is her main goal.

Even when they crack and they break,
And it makes her heart sad and ache,
to her they are still a treasure.
Their worth is not even possible to measure.

With these Christmas dishes,
all she wishes
is for another year with them all.
Life hasn't been easy, but she still moves forward
standing strong, standing tall.

With these Christmas dishes,
she also wishes is for relief from her pain,
Since having lost loved ones, makes it hard for
happiness to remain.

But the love she has for her family and friends will be
what keeps her going through the years, until the
years end.

After we finished, there was complete silence for what felt like an eternity and it was unnerving. Relief came when I heard people clapping and whistling. As the crowd continued to applaud and then honor us with a standing ovation, I realized we did good. We did real good!

The four of us took a bow and Anna came to the stage area to take us to our table. Gene, Greg, Michele, Terry and Charles Watkins all stood up as we came over to be seated. They hugged and kissed us and adorned us with wonderful compliments for our performance. Gene said he would like to introduce us to some dear friends that he asked to come to the event. First was a couple, Dan and Lori Manno and their friend, Todd Higby who was Michele's step-brother and a judge for the Ontario County courts. They were all so gracious to us. Johnny and Maria filled in the empty seats. It was heart-warming to be surrounded by all of these new people who were so welcoming of me and my people. We all exchanged introductions and pleasantries. However, with so many people coming up to our table to congratulate us on our performance, it was too difficult to have meaningful conversations.

Maria was sitting a couple of tables away with Ella and Noah. She was smiling and holding hands with her new friends. I was relieved to see she wasn't carrying the weight of our conversation from a couple days ago, on her shoulders. The three of them were in their own little world. A kind, unsegregated world.

I was pumped up with adrenaline after performing our set and very thirsty. The waitress came over to me and asked me if I would like a whiskey – neat. I even surprised myself when I told her that I would prefer just a glass of grape juice and some water. I sat there for a few minutes just taking all of it in. Since I had never performed anywhere other than NOLA, this was a new experience. In the South, where I was from, it wasn't unusual to have colored singers and musicians performing at different establishments. African Americans were allowed much more freedom because of the racial demographics in southern Louisiana in general and NOLA in particular. Although our racial segregation laws were more lenient than other parts of Louisiana, they still restricted the lives of black people. It was unfair and unjust and made us feel substandard. So, there I was in the North East where I wasn't sure my family and I would be as easily accepted. My fears and insecurities all subsided that afternoon at the Jazz Jam. We were embraced and welcomed into the Naples community; we were accepted at par.

Anna arranged for a local band to perform after we were done. They finished setting up their instruments and the music started to flow. I was surprised at how good they were! They played popular tunes and people started dancing. What happened next, was beyond surprising. Anna and Peter went to the dance floor and all eyes were on the two of them. I remembered Phillip told me that Anna was a wonderful dancer. But I have to say, she was spectacular! Her body moved gracefully with a hint of sexiness. Peter was also very good but it was Anna who stole the show! The two of them stayed on the dance floor for a couple of songs and then came back to our area. All of us at our table got up and gave the two of them a round of applause. I could see that Anna was in her element and very appreciative of the accolades. She sat down next to me and said, "Pierre, it has been life-changing having you and your family with us this past week. We feel that you have made it possible for our community to embrace us once again, the way it was before Phillip killed Carmelita. It is amazing to me how music can unite people and we are indebted to you." Tears welled up in my eyes and I told Anna that I too had much to be thankful for, starting with her and Peter. I said, "Anna, the two of you made our stay in Naples the best time my family and I ever had since we became a family. Although we are not connected to you by blood, we are connected by love and respect. We are family."

Maria, Ella and Noah were also dancing. Even Greg and Michele were out there cutting a rug. Sadly, it was getting close to the end of the Jazz Jam. The band announced they would be playing a slow song for their finale. Greg asked Michele to dance and Anna and Peter were back on the dance floor. Gene then asked me if I would dance with him. I was hoping that he would and I gladly accepted his invitation. He took my hand and led me to the dance floor. Gene wasn't the smoothest dancer but he held his own. I could tell he was nervous and not sure of his moves on many levels. To put him at ease, I took over the lead and he was a great follower. I didn't see it coming when at the end of the song, he took me in a stronghold, dipped me backwards and pulled me tightly to him. He then whispered in my ear, "I hope you see that at times I can follow, but at times I too can lead. Thank you Pierre for this first of hopefully many dances." I stood there stunned, as my heart was rapidly beating, my head was reeling and I had feelings stirring inside of me that hadn't been awakened in quite some time. Gene escorted me back to my seat at the table and excused himself to get a drink. My mouth was open to speak, however, he was gone before I could even get any words out. Even if I could have spoken to him, I wouldn't have known what to say; I was speechless! A waitress walked by and I breathlessly asked her if I could have a whiskey - neat, as soon as possible!

All of us lingered downstairs for a couple of hours after the Jazz Jam was over, having a great time. However, we realized we needed to go up to our rooms so my people could start getting ready for their trip back to NOLA in the morning. Everyone who was originally at our table was still there, except Terry, who was busy seeing to the cleanup of the room. Charles Watkins had overindulged in the wine during the afternoon, and was talking to everyone at the table, a bit too loudly. I suggested food and some coffee for all of us. I did it that way so that Charles could sober up a bit without anything having to be said specifically to him. Anna looked over at me with gratitude in her eyes. I could tell she was embarrassed by his behavior, but she too didn't want to draw any attention to a situation that could potentially unfold.

Johnny and Tee evaluated the situation and went to Terry and asked her if she could set up a separate table for Maria, Noah and Ella. They didn't want the children to be in earshot of grown-up talk, if grown-up talk needed to be used. Peter said he would be taking Charles home after they were done eating. He too realized that Charles was in no shape to drive.

Charles came over and asked Gene if he could sit next to me for a minute. He said he needed to talk to me. Gene asked me if I was comfortable with that. I wanted to defuse the situation, so I said that would be fine. I couldn't imagine what he could possibly want to talk to me about as I hardly knew him, although I had met him a few times during Phillip's trial. However, he wasn't Phillip's attorney because he did not specialize in criminal law. All I knew about him from Phillip was that he was close friends of his parents, practiced family law, handled the Wilcoxs' will and was involved in the payout to Angela Caprizzi (GG).

When Charles sat next to me, I could see he was upset so I asked him what was wrong. Was there something I could help him with? He was completely intoxicated. All I could understand was him saying, "Forgive me, Father, for I have sinned." Thankfully the food we ordered was served. I made sure that Charles ate some. He was like a child. I told him to drink some water along with his meal. It didn't make any sense to try and have an intelligent conversation with him. I told him I would be staying in Naples for at least another week and I would come and see him. That seemed to pacify him. When he was almost done eating, Peter came over and said he would be taking Charles home as it was getting late.

I was intrigued and confused as to why Charles would make that specific statement; the very same words written on the bottom corner of the wall in the berry-picker house. I always thought it was Phillip who wrote that. But now, I started to think it might have been Charles who had written it. Was he trying to tell me something? It made me wonder what it was about me that made people feel comfortable sharing their secrets. It became a blessing and a curse. After my people were gone, I would definitely be going to see Charles.

After Charles and Peter left, we all finished our meal. We said goodbye to all of our new friends. I could tell Maria was sad to be leaving Ella and Noah. Kelly and John saw us to the lobby. They thanked us all for the wonderful performance and wished safe travels to Johnny, Tee, Maria and Greg. Terry came up to me and gave me a big bear hug. I was a bit surprised but hugged her back just as tight. She said, "You and Gene looked like you truly enjoy each other's company. It made me happy to see him smile and you are the reason for that. Thank you for bringing enjoyment to my brother's life!

Gene and Anna were leaving to drive back to the grape farm. However, before they pulled away, Gene kissed my hand and said he looked forward to seeing me over the next week if my schedule allowed. He knew that in two days I would be moving from the Naples Hotel to the grape farm for the rest of my stay in Naples. He suggested we could take some walks through the vineyard and maybe go into the town of Canandaigua for lunch or dinner. My mind went back to our dance at the Naples Hotel and made me long to be in his arms again and close to his heart and body. I needed to be physically connected to him again to see where things could possibly go between the two of us. I replied, "That would be nice. But perhaps one evening we could move some of the furniture in the living room off to the side and we could dance again." Gene just chuckled and said that sounded good but he would be doing the leading next time. Laughing and with a wink, I responded, "We'll see about that Gene."

Greg told us he was going to be taking Michele home. He said he would see all of us early in the morning. I hugged Michele and told her I hoped to see her before I headed back to NOLA in a couple of weeks. She was a good match for Greg as she kept him on his toes and he seemed enthralled with her. Here we were hundreds of miles away from home and both of us met someone in Naples, NY! I was getting excited to think of what the future might hold for both Greg and me with our newly found friendships.

Johnny, Tee and Maria walked me to my room. Heartache was setting in with their upcoming departure. I kissed them all good night and thanked them for their wonderful performances at the Jazz Jam. Johnny responded, "It is us who have to thank you for this most wonderful time in Naples. We met people and saw things that would never have happened in our lives if not for you. We are blessed and we love you." I was very emotional and couldn't even think of the right words to say, so I said nothing. Instead, I just nodded my head, placed my hand on my heart, and touched each of them.

Sleep did not come easily as my mind was swirling with thoughts from our amazing day. Eventually, I fell asleep through pure exhaustion but not before saying a little prayer of thanks for having met a genuinely good man. Unlike, TCA who never proposed a romantic relationship with me, Gene seemed to be taking that initiative.

I awoke very early in the morning and got dressed. When I went downstairs, I was surprised to see Terry hurriedly setting up a table with coffee and scones. She said she thought we might like to have a little something to eat before we were picked up to go to the train station. There were also two bags of food that she brought over to me. Terry said, "I packed up some sandwiches for your family's train ride. I also heard that Maria liked grape pie, so there are a few slices in there for her." I expressed my gratitude to Terry for her kindness and generosity. I sat down for a cup of coffee and was pleased when all of my people joined me at the table. Everyone was dressed and ready to go. We quickly had our breakfast together. Johnny and Greg already moved all of their luggage down into the lobby. It really hit me hard when I saw all of them put on their Ellis jackets; they would be leaving me. We gathered all of their belongings and went outside to wait for our rides to the station.

It was a whirlwind week but a wonderful week. It was the first time Johnny and I had a chance to bond.

Back in NOLA, everything was always so rushed, with rehearsing or singing at different clubs with our band. We never had time to just stop and smell the roses. Having spent the week in Naples without as many commitments or responsibilities, we were able to stop and smell the grapes instead. It was a new experience for me to actually be able to live in the moment and just appreciate being with each other.

Anna and Peter brought two automobiles when they picked us up at the Naples Hotel. Greg was glad to have one last time to drive his borrowed vehicle to the train station. He again took Johnny, Tee and Maria. Anna, Peter and I drove in the other. They knew I would want to be there at the station to see my people off. I hugged all of them and said I would see them probably in a week or two. Maria needed to get back to school and I could tell Johnny was anxious to get back to work with the band. Also, Tee had several singing lessons set up for the next week at *Liberté*, the business that my friend Li'lM and she now owned. It was an extraordinary getaway for them, but they had to return to their lives in NOLA.

As Johnny, Tee, Maria and Greg were waving to me from the train, I remembered a quote I read by poet Rudyard Kipling, "The strength of the pack is the wolf and the strength of the wolf is the pack." I found my pack, and I would be their strength just as they were mine. I blew them all a kiss and got into Anna's auto. She explained that Peter had to be getting back to their home in Geneva so she would be dropping me off at the hotel.

GIRL TALK

I planned to stay at the Naples Hotel for one more evening before going to the grape farm for at least another week. I was thrilled when Anna asked me if I would mind if she spent my last evening at the Naples Hotel with me. I have to admit I didn't want to be alone. I said to Anna, "Nothing could make me happier. Thank you for knowing the night would be hard without my people around me. But Anna, you need to know, I also consider you one of my people." When we pulled into the parking area for the hotel, Anna pulled out a little overnight bag she had packed just in case I would take her up on her offer.

That evening, Anna had a bottle of whiskey and a bottle of vodka sent to my room. She also took the liberty of ordering room service, rather than having to go downstairs. She expressed a desire to have a meaningful conversation. I was glad we were going to be able to open up to each other without being disturbed or overheard.

We finished our dinner and Anna took our drinks

over to the couch in the little parlor area. She said, "Please tell me about your life when you were young Pierre, if you are comfortable doing so. Whatever is shared tonight between the two of us will not leave this room." The shot of whiskey I quickly downed gave me freedom of speech…

"Anna, I was born and grew up in Mississippi. I lived there with my mother and her husband Damas DuMonde. Damas was my stepfather and he was wonderful to me and treated me as if I were his own daughter. My birth father died when I was young. He was working for Damas as his right-hand man on the cotton crops at the Diamond Dust Plantation that Damas owned. I had heard the rumors that perhaps the accident that killed my father wasn't an accident but I never wanted to believe that. Some people said that when my father and Damas were out evaluating the cotton crops, a widow maker tree limb broke off from a large tree and fell in front of the horse my father was riding on. It caused the horse to go up on his hind legs and my father fell off and cracked open his skull. Damas took care of all of the arrangements for my father's funeral. Not long after that, my mother became the lady of the house at the Diamond Dust Plantation and willingly shared a bed with the man of the house.

The upbringing I had on the Diamond Dust Plantation was amazing. I felt I was blessed to be living a life of privilege. My mother's name was Amelia and she loved me very much. She and I would do many things together, especially around the holidays. She had a sweet voice and we would sing together while setting our elegant table for the holidays, using her cherished Christmas dishes that were passed down to her from her mother. We would have our neighbors and friends gather at our house for scrumptious meals. Mother would play the piano and I would sing popular songs from the mid-1800s. People were astonished by my voice and enjoyed the performances we would put on for them.

After one of our performances, I was inspired to write my poem "Christmas Dishes" to honor my mother. The following holiday season when I recited the poem at one of our gatherings, the group of friends all marveled at how beautiful it was. I decided that night, when I was older, I would turn my poem into a song.

All was well in my life. However, that all changed when I started to become a young woman. At that time, Damas started to ravage me. That is what I called his rapes. I had developed early and had a voluptuous body for a 13-year-old. Each time I was ravaged by him, what I did to protect myself - protect my sanity - was a ritual I called "frozen." I would start at the top of my head with my open hand and move it over my face, down over my heart and down to my private parts, chanting to myself, frozen, frozen, frozen.

After the ravagings, I referred to him as D. The D stood for devil and that is what he became to me.

Strangely, after each of these ravagings, he would give me an impressive piece of jewelry. When he requested I wear the latest piece of jewelry to our next social event, I believe he re-lived his thrill. For me, it didn't minimize what he did to me, but I was astute enough to know not to let those jewels out of my sight.

As a result of D's ravagings, I became pregnant. He sent me away to the Ursuline Convent in New Orleans, which was also a home for unwed mothers, to have my child. D told me my baby would be given up for adoption. I was so young and had no say in the matter. My mother was so sick, that I don't think she had the strength to question D's decision, although I knew she was heartbroken I was being sent away. By the grace of God, the head nun at the convent, Sister Veronica found out how I came to be with child. I was crying about my situation and she overheard me. She did not originally know my circumstances. But when she found them out, she said she could make it possible for me to escape my life as I had known it, and start a new life living with her sister, Miss Margaret. She told me I would need to make my decision quickly.

Totally at a loss as to what to do, I went to St. Louis Cathedral and said a prayer. Hurriedly I walked out of the church and through Jackson Square. While I was in the middle of it, I looked up to the heavens and said to myself that I would spin around seven times and then open my eyes. Depending on the direction I would be facing when I opened them, that would determine my destiny. If I wound up facing the Mississippi River, it was a sign from God that I would return home to Mississippi and be with my mother. However, I feared that the ravagings of D would still be part of my future. But if I wound up facing any of the other three streets, it was meant to be that I would go in a different direction in my life. I closed my eyes and spun around seven times. When I opened them, I wasn't facing the Mississippi! It was the most pivotal moment in my life. From that moment on, the child Maria Pierre Quinones was gone and the young woman "Pierre" emerged. It felt like I was a butterfly going through a metamorphosis. Going forward, I never told anyone my real name. I simply became Pierre Louis. Since the St. Louis Cathedral was the place where I felt most safe, I decided making my last name "Louis" was apropos.

With my newly found lease on life, I ran back to the Ursuline Convent and told Sister Veronica that I gratefully would accept her offer and move in with Miss Margaret.

When the handler from Mississippi came to take me back home, Sister Veronica staged it to make it look like I ran away. She was willing to accept the wrath of the fallout of my disappearance. I was discretely moved into Miss Margaret's home which was called the Courtesan Cottage. It was a house of ill repute. However, I was never expected to be in that line of work. To be able to stay there, I agreed to do the cooking, cleaning and laundry.

I grew to love the ladies I was living with at the cottage, especially Miss Margaret. They were all so good to me. I learned so much about the real world by listening to their experiences and just sharing our lives. Erina, Irene, Dee and Holly were the ladies of the house and Miss Margaret was something like their talent agent. In reality, she was the Madam of the cottage. She would book their engagements for dinners, lavish balls and other events where men would pay a large amount of money to have a beautiful woman on their arm. Miss Margaret was paid by the ladies for that service. However, what the ladies chose to do after those services were rendered, she did not involve herself in. I remembered thinking to myself that since I had lived in both, there was not much difference between a whore house and a convent – one tends to the needs of the body and the other to the needs of the soul.

The ladies of the Courtesan Cottage became my new family as I promised Sister Veronica I would never try and contact my mother. It would be too risky and might make it possible for D to find me.

After a couple of months, Sister Veronica came to me to tell me she learned my mother passed away from Tuberculosis. All I could do was offer up a prayer for her and light a candle at the St. Louis Cathedral. I remember when I was forced to leave her and come to NOLA to have my child, she looked so frail from the disease. I thanked God that her suffering had come to an end but it truly saddened me; not only had I lost my son but also my mother in a relatively short period. It left my heart heavy.

Time went by and I was getting acclimated to my new life at the cottage. It was known around our area that I had a great singing voice. So, Miss Margaret had me singing in different saloons and brothels close to the cottage. I was nervous at first, but as I got to know the ladies in the different houses and the madams, my fears subsided. These women were just trying to survive and make the best of the circumstances they were dealt.

Some of the clients who visited these establishments thought I was there for their pleasure. However, it was made very clear that I was only at these places to sing. Word traveled fast about my voice and I was asked to perform at quite a few establishments around the city. It was about that time when I first met TCA.

TCA's full name was Timothy C. Anderson. He was an Irishman with a handlebar mustache and a full head of thick hair. The rumors around NOLA were that at a young age, he started as a hustler working both with the police and against them in the same transactions. At times he went to the *demimonde* side – the half world. He would portray himself as a politician and a pillar of society but he would dabble in and derive profit from drugs and gambling. However, his largest investment was in prostitution. He was even referred to as the mayor of Storyville.

When I was still in my teens, Miss Margaret told me I would become a singer for a local band that TCA put together. But first, he wanted to hear my voice to see if he would take me under his wing as something of a manager. TCA took the liberty of assigning a handler to take me to and from all of my performances. His name was Frankie. At first, I was not welcoming of this perceived intrusion into my life. However, as time went by, Frankie became my best friend.

Frankie escorted me on the first night to meet my new band members. Our first rehearsal went very well. I came up with, The Lagniappe Orchestra, as our stage name. Lagniappe means a little something extra and I felt that was exactly what we were. That night, I met TCA for the first time. He was a freckled Irishman who I thought was good-looking and had an air about him that I was drawn to.

Our band practiced together for several days and the members embraced me as one of their own. We were magical and we were ready for our opening night.

I was busy getting myself prepared physically and emotionally for our big show. A box from a local shop that catered to high-end clothing arrived at our front door. Inside was the most beautiful green dress I had ever seen! There was also a black satchel containing a lovely necklace with three strands of glass beads with the colors of NOLA. There was a note that read, "You are to wear this when you perform for the first time at my pleasure club. In exchange for this opportunity I am providing you with, you are to be available to me when I want to hear an angel sing." It was signed, "TCA."

Opening night was incredible. But what mattered most to me that evening was that Miss Margaret and my friends -   Erina, Irene, Holly and Dee, who I lovingly referred to as the Courtesan Cottage Clandestines (CC's) were there to share in my success. And the greatest surprise of the night was when a woman came over and hugged and kissed me. Her gestures surprised me and I took a step back from her. It was when I looked into her eyes that I realized who the woman was. It was Sister Veronica in regular clothes and not her nun habit!

From that day forward, the Lagniappe Orchestra and I played at TCA's pleasure clubs or wherever he made arrangements for us to perform. Without fail, Frankie would come and escort me to and from every performance. This arrangement went on for many years. Since Frankie and I spent so much time together, we learned about each other's lives. I eventually opened up to him about how I was ravaged by D and as a result, I became pregnant. Frankie was one of the few people who knew I had to give up my son and how that broke my heart.

My life was very busy and somewhat full. After a few years, I was blessed to open up my own business called *Liberté* with my friend and business partner, Li'lM. *Liberté* means freedom and at that point in my life, I was free from many things that had held me back.

At *Liberté*, we offered singing and piano lessons. Our business was in the French Quarter and quite successful. During that time, I first met my son, Johnny, obviously not knowing he was my son. He was in his teens and was introduced to Li'lM and myself by a woman named Flordie. One day she came and asked us if we would provide lessons to four youngsters who were attending school nearby and living in the neighborhood. She explained they couldn't afford the regular cost of our singing and piano lessons but felt they deserved a chance at trying to better their lives by attending our classes and being inspired by us. We agreed to take these students under our wings and loved spending time with them. The four students were Johnny, Tee, Chester and Faith. Chester and Faith were brother and sister. Johnny was the oldest of the group by quite a few years. He seemed to be their protector and leader and he definitely took a shine to the dark-haired girl named Tee. That is how my Johnny and Tee met and they have been together ever since. Li'lM and I referred to the four of them as our YP's (young proteges) and we couldn't have been prouder of them!

At that time, I had no idea Johnny was my son but after having met him, I longed to find my own son who I thought had been adopted. For several years, I made inquiries but was not successful in finding out his whereabouts or who may have adopted him. It was gut-wrenching to learn that the entire time I was searching for my son, he was already part of my life. It wasn't until Greg started to look into background information for the articles he wrote about me for the *New Orleans Observer* that I found out the truth about what happened to my son. It was Greg who brought Johnny and me together. Through Greg's investigative work, my prayers had been answered. However, there were things that I never wanted to be made public knowledge. That included exactly who Johnny's father was and the circumstances of how he came to be my son. Greg learned that D was involved with a woman named Jennifer Lacoste who was from New Orleans. She was D's *placage* wife. *Placage* was a recognized extralegal system where ethnic European men would enter into a common-law marriage arrangement with non-Europeans of African or mixed-race ancestry.

Instead of putting my son, his son, up for adoption, he had Jennifer raise the boy. However, after D's death in the brothel accident, his money was no longer coming her way. Greg speculated that she did not want the financial responsibility of taking care of the boy but she was compassionate enough to let Johnny continue to live under her roof. He was not loved and was left on his own for the most part.

I haven't asked Johnny to share any information on his upbringing; it just hasn't been the right time. Or maybe it will be a discussion we never have. I didn't want to be responsible for bringing any more heartache or strife into his life. That is why I only agreed to Greg publishing the articles about me if he left out certain information I told him he could not include. Greg agreed to my request. I trust him with my deepest secrets and I now also trust you with them."

AFFAIRS OF THE HEART

An hour had gone by telling Anna my life story. Our drinks were empty, so we refilled our glasses and Anna said, "Please tell me more. Your life is fascinating to me. However, I am sad that you never talked about finding love. I hope that is forthcoming." I reflected for a minute before I was able to continue. A few tears streamed down my face before I found the strength to tell Anna about Father Tommy.

"Yes Anna, there were men in my life but nothing serious. I had needs just like any woman and they were taken care of. However, I never gave my heart to anyone. That was until I met a man named Father Tommy Mulroney. He was the priest at the Saint Louis Cathedral where I attended church on Sundays. We started to speak to each other after Mass while sitting on a bench in Jackson Square. At first, I was so nervous to even speak to him, but then after a few weeks, it was the only thing I wanted to do. He was knowledgeable about so many things including music and was everything I wanted in a man.

Father Tommy shared with me that even from a young age, he knew he wanted to be a servant of the Lord. So, at times, I felt guilty that I may have been distracting him from performing God's work. I had conflicting emotions about our somewhat innocent relationship but I couldn't stay away from him. I never felt this way about another man before. With everything I went through with D, I never thought I would be unfrozen. Sadly, Father Tommy unfroze my heart. We never did anything other than talk and hold hands and I didn't push him for more. Our hand-holding affair went on for three months. I was in love with him and I felt he loved me back. Unfortunately for me, he was reassigned to a church back in Ireland, where he was originally from. He said he couldn't refuse the transfer as it had been decided by the higher-ranking members of the Catholic Church. When he finished giving me the news, I put my head down and took his hand that had been in mine and made him feel the tears welling out of my eyes.

Father Tommy was the first real love of my life and I lost him. Another man in my life was my protector, Frankie. Although I wouldn't say he was a love of my life, I loved and cared for that man deeply. I knew he had feelings for me but he would never dare initiate a romantic relationship. His loyalties belonged to TCA first and foremost. I had lost Father Tommy and Frankie within a short period. Frankie was killed in a roofing accident while repairing a house that had been damaged due to a fire. It did hurt me to know that Frankie knew Johnny was my son and he also knew about TCA sending Father Tommy away. I want to think he didn't do anything about either of those matters as his hands were tied, or he didn't know what to do about them before his unexpected death. Like so many things in my life, I have had to accept that I will never know those answers.

With the two most important men in my life being gone from me, I was lonelier than I had ever been; I was a hollow woman.

The other love of my life was TCA. From the first time I met TCA when he kissed my hand, through my life and until his death, I loved the man. Even though he was old enough to be my father, I could have been in love with him if he ever opened that door. The last time he saw me, he said, "Pierre, I find it hard to leave your presence, but have never trusted myself to stay there for too long as I may have not ever been able to walk away from you." He put me on a pedestal and I wanted to stay there. I desired to be his everything but I never became his anything. If not for TCA, I would not have had my career, the legal rights to my song "Lace Around the Moon" and *Liberté* with Li'l M. Our relationship endured the test of time without ever testing the waters of what might have been.

TCA told me the relationship he had with me was the most fulfilling and cherished one in his life. He never wanted to ruin that for himself. He once told my friend Flordie that if you truly love someone you don't make them your own, you set them free. And that is what he did with me. He even went so far as to purchase a burial crypt for me next to his family crypt in the Metairie Cemetery. It was so odd to me that he did that and I couldn't believe his gesture. Was that selfish or selfless? I could only assume that since he couldn't or wouldn't be with me during his lifetime, we would be close together for eternity after we both passed. There is no way I will ever know what his thought process was, but I have the legal documentation that shows I have ownership of the crypt. However, being buried next to him is not where I want my body to be laid to rest. Rather, I intended to purchase my own family crypt for my newly found family; they are the ones I want to spend eternity next to.

It wasn't until recently that I learned it was TCA who orchestrated Father Tommy's departure back to Ireland. Greg found a letter in Frankie's personal items from the Archdiocese of New Orleans. The letter was to formalize that Father Tommy Mulroney was to be reassigned back to

Ireland and thanked Timothy C. Anderson for paying for his transportation to be with his sickly father. Although it gave me some closure in knowing Father Tommy may have never left me if it had not been for TCA's involvement, it left my heart empty. I despised TCA after learning of his role in Father Tommy's departure but still loved him even after his passing. With TCA there were so many secrets, so many lies all to disguise the truths he tried to hide. The relationship I had with him was the most convoluted relationship I ever had. Anna, you now know all about my affairs of the heart."

Anna said, "No wonder the articles Greg did on you for the *New Orleans Observer* are called the "Perseverance of Pierre." I have to say, Pierre, that is a perfect way to describe you and your life. You are an amazing woman." She reached for my hands and held them. She looked me in the eyes and said, "Pierre, I believe if you keep an open heart, true love will fill it. You may find it back in NOLA or down the road at a grape farm."

The whiskey and vodka had lost their appeal so I poured us both a glass of water. At that point, I was emotionally spent from telling Anna about my life. However, I wanted to learn more about her. I said, "Anna would you be willing to tell me about your life? There is so little I know about you. Please let me get to know you as you have become a daughter to me."

Surprisingly, Anna opened up and said, "I hope you don't find me to be ungrateful for all I have been blessed to have. Other than what happened with Phillip, my life has been wonderful. It's just that I wish my mother had been more like you." Anna then started to cry. I reached out and held her hand and asked her if she was okay. She told me that other than Peter, she didn't have anyone to talk to about anything. She lost touch with her high school friends when she moved to Geneva to be with Peter. Then it became difficult for her to maintain her other friendships due to some people in the Naples community disliking her because she was Phillip's twin.

Anna went on to explain that growing up, she never really felt comfortable sharing many things with her mother and especially not her father. Anna said, "To be honest Pierre, I did love my father but I never felt close to him. Don't get me wrong, he was a good father in terms of providing for me and being present in my life. However, I don't recall ever having an in-depth conversation with him about anything; he was aloof. I may have only been imagining it, but I didn't feel we had the father-daughter relationship that some of my friends had with their fathers; we were not connected.

Our mother was more affectionate with Phillip and me than our father was. In retrospect, I truly believe she loved us and she showed us with her constant hugs and kisses. Phillip and I were her pride and joy and she was very involved in our lives growing up. However, it sometimes felt superficial to me; the appearance of a perfect family was more important than actually being a family. I also felt like she too was not totally connected to us. Since Peter and I have been blessed to have baby Pierre and Phillip, the connection we have to these two new humans we created is all-encompassing. They are the most important aspects of our lives. And now Pierre that you have your son Johnny, I think you know about the love I am talking about. It is the greatest and most rewarding of all. There was just something missing in our family dynamics. I just couldn't put my finger on what was amiss."

When Anna was done revealing her most heartfelt insecurities to me, I said, "The conversation we had has been healing. We both have issues we are going to be dealing with for the rest of our lives; we get each other Anna. I want you to know I have not talked to a friend like this since I was with my CC's many years ago. Unfortunately, Holly passed away and I have lost touch with Irene, Erina and Dee over the years. That's just how life goes. Let's get some sleep and I believe in the morning things will be easier for both of us knowing that we are there for each other – whatever comes our way."

The following morning, Anna and I woke up close to

noon! We obviously needed sleep after our long night of bonding. Both of us needed coffee, so I went downstairs and asked to have some sent to the room. Since I already had most of my clothes packed, it only took me a few minutes to put together the rest of my luggage. After we dressed, we went down to the lobby. Terry was working the front desk and I asked her for my bill for the two rooms I had for the week. The amount was quite a bit less than I anticipated. I asked her if there was an error on the bill. She just winked at me and said the hotel owners, Kelly and John, were so pleased and thankful for our Jazz Jam performance that they wanted to make it up to me in some way. That was their way. I asked her to please thank them for their generosity and tell them I would like to stop in to see them before I go back to NOLA.

Anna dropped me off at the grape farm. Gene came out when he saw Anna's auto pull into the driveway. He insisted on carrying all my luggage to the bedroom I would be using for my stay. While Gene was taking in my belongings, Anna asked me what I would like to do with the additional week I would be spending in Naples. I told her I would love to spend some time with her babies. She said that would be great and would let me know when she would bring them to the grape farm for a visit.

I also asked her if she would take me to meet with

Charles Watkins at his law office the following day. With what happened after the Jazz Jam, I felt it imperative to talk with him about what he said when he was sitting next to me. However, I wanted to have a private conversation with him, without Anna or anyone else overhearing what would be discussed. Anna said she would drop me off there the following morning and asked if an hour would be enough time. Thinking that since all I wanted to know was why he said, "Forgive me, Father, for I have sinned," I told her an hour would be plenty of time.

To get a better understanding of who exactly Charles Watkins was, I asked Anna to fill me in a bit on him and his life. She explained that not only was he her parents' attorney, but he was also their friend. Anna said, "Charles always seemed to be at all of our holiday get-togethers and family events. His generosity of gifts was embarrassing at times. Whatever Phillip and I wanted and our parents couldn't afford, Charles would purchase for us. He was married, however, he and his wife never had children. I never inquired if that was their choice or God's will. Unfortunately, his wife passed away several years ago. She was sickly for many years but I didn't know what her ailment was. I feel bad for telling you this since it was only idle gossip, but there were hushed rumors that he may have been involved with a man years ago. And even if the rumors were true, I believe we should all be able to be who we are and live our lives without judgment. Everyone has secrets and God knows there were enough secrets in my life.

Charles was also not in the best of health. For as long as I knew him, he had diabetes and he didn't take care of himself health-wise. His drinking didn't help. He seemed to always be drowning his sorrows. I remember growing up, he always seemed so sad and lonely. But he is a good man and always found the time to volunteer at our local hospital and charity events. He has been a part of my life for as long as I can remember."

My last request of Anna was for her to take me to the train station in the next day or two so I could purchase my return ticket home to NOLA. I told her another week in Naples would be wonderful. However, I needed to get back to reality and spend time with my people and my city. I was longing for them.

After Anna left, Gene and I sat down to eat an early supper of roasted lamb, baby potatoes and green beans that he had prepared for us before he headed back out to tend to the fields. I thanked him for the delicious meal and told him how much I appreciated him taking the time to make sure I was well-fed. He could see how exhausted I was, so he kissed me on the cheek and said good-night. Once in bed, I could hardly keep my eyes open and sleep came as soon as I laid down my head.

When I woke up the following morning, I was revived. The smell of fresh coffee brewing was so inviting. I quickly dressed and went to the kitchen where there were some tasty treats on the table. Looking out the window, I could see Gene working among the grapevines. He was such a hard-working man but he also had a soft side to him. I looked forward to my week at the grape farm with him. Not long after I finished my coffee, Anna pulled into the driveway.

FORGIVE ME, FATHER,
FOR I HAVE SINNED

Anna dropped me off at Charles Watkins' office. Upon entering, his secretary recognized me and said she would let him know I was there. Charles came out and escorted me to his office area. He looked sheepish as he motioned for me to sit at his small conference table and quickly apologized for his behavior at the Naples Hotel. He said, "Miss Pierre, please forgive me for the deplorable way I acted. I had been drinking heavily that day and was not in my right mind when I was talking to you. If I said something to offend you, I apologize."

I told Charles that I wasn't there to discuss his intoxication remorse but rather the words he said to me. He acted as if he didn't know what I was talking about. That may have been true but I wasn't going to let the conversation end there. I said, "Charles, what did you mean when you said, "Forgive me, Father, for I have sinned?" The color drained from his face and he looked as though he might get sick. Charles quickly reached for the bowl of blueberries that were on the table and started to eat them with a glass of water. He explained that he has diabetes and the blueberries help stabilize his blood sugar levels. After a couple of minutes, he seemed more composed and said, "I never wanted to have this conversation with anyone. But my stupidity has caused a door to be opened that I believe can no longer stay shut. What I am about to tell you can never be shared with anyone. It would only hurt someone who I believe you and I love, as well as destroy the reputations of good families, including my own." He got up from the table and went and poured two glasses of water. After he took a couple sips, tears started flowing. I could see the turmoil he was in and I felt sorry for him. All I could think of to say to him was, "Charles, I think you know that I have kept all of the secrets Phillip shared with me since my first meeting him about 20 years ago. That is why I think you want to tell me something; I can be trusted."

Charles seemed to be comforted by my words. He gained the strength he needed and said, "I don't know how much Phillip or Anna told you about their parents, Henry and Lillian. But I will tell you they were good people. I was not only their family attorney, but the three of us were very good friends since grammar school. My wife Mary, God rest her soul, was also friends with them. Although, she didn't spend as much time as I did socializing with them, she never begrudged me for wanting to. Mary and I had a marriage of convenience. She was a wonderful woman, however, our relationship was not physical. I was not attracted to her, but we were the best of friends although we were not in love. We stayed together because we deeply cared for one another; it worked for us and we were able to portray ourselves as a happily married couple to our church and community.

Henry, Lillian and I would get together quite often at their home and share drinks and meals together. They had a beautiful home and vineyard. They were well off financially, but they never flaunted their money. Instead, they were constantly giving back to their community. Their lives were full although their hearts were empty. The thing they wanted most but couldn't have, was a child. They tried for many years, but it seemed like it was not going to happen for them.

A few years went by and the three of us spent even more time together. There was one evening when we overindulged in a great deal of wine. I admit I may have had a crush on Lillian. However, I never was inappropriate or flirtatious with her. I respected Henry and our friendship was too important to me to ever risk jeopardizing it. So, what happened next, totally took me by surprise. While we were sitting in the parlor, Lillian said they had one last option to possibly have a child. Henry interjected,

"Charles, there is no proper way for us to ask you to do something unethical, immoral and perhaps even illegal, so I am just going to say it. Lillian and I would be forever indebted to you if you would be intimate with her so she could possibly conceive a child. We know what we are asking of you is unscrupulous and selfish on our part. However, you are the only person we trust enough to ask for this precious gift; you are our last hope."

Their outlandish request left me stunned. After it sank in, I realized that Henry was permitting me to commit adultery with his wife. In fact, I was being asked to. Since I knew that Mary and I would never have children, I entertained the thought. It took me a few minutes to work it out in my mind that this would be a very special gift I could give to them. Then with the courage of more wine, I agreed to their indecent proposal. They were both so appreciative but also made me promise this would be something that would never be shared outside of our circle of three. I told them it would remain our secret. Lillian started to cry and said she couldn't even begin to thank me for what I was doing for her and Henry.

That same evening, thankfully still intoxicated, Lillian and I went down to the berry-picker house. On the bed in the first room, we didn't make love, but hopefully life. After Lillian left to go back to Henry, I felt terrible for what I had just done. There was a pencil on a table in the room that the migrant workers used to sign their names on the wall and leave little messages. As a way to relieve myself of some of the guilt I felt, I too went to the wall and left the message, "Forgive me, Father, for I have sinned."

We all waited a month to see if Lillian was with child; she was not.

Lillian and I repeated our first night, once a month for the next two consecutive months.

Although I believe it broke Henry's heart to see me go down to the berry-picker house where Lillian would be waiting, he never said a word. He loved Lillian so much that he wanted her to have the opportunity to have the one thing he didn't seem to be able to give her. Henry gave his wife to me so my seed could fill her empty womb and give her what she coveted. I assumed he did this because he felt he owed her that since his seed may have been useless to her. What we did was taking a risk on many levels.

Four months into our arrangement, they had me over to their house for dinner. Lillian had prepared a delicious supper. While we were eating, Henry poured two glasses of wine. One for me and one for him. However, Lillian had a glass of grape juice. Henry proposed a toast. He said, "To our dearest friend Charles. Because of you, our lives will forever be full. Lillian is with child."

Charles breathed a sigh of relief when he finished

getting out what was obviously on his mind and soul for the past 35 years. He said, "Miss Pierre, you have to understand I was shocked with the news. It was one thing to think it could happen, but when it became an actuality, I was conflicted. We all believed that since Lillian became pregnant while I was having relations with her, the baby she was carrying was mine, not Henry's. After a few months went by, it started to sink in that I was going to be the biological father. I started to embrace the idea of fatherhood. However, I had to quickly squelch those feelings and accept I would never have a claim to the child. A promise is a promise.

We continued to get together for dinners for the next several months. However, we never discussed our agreement. As it was getting closer to Lillian's delivery date, our times together became less frequent and then not at all. Henry did promise me he would let me know once the child was born. However, he asked me to not come to the hospital. They felt the experience was something only he and Lillian should share; I was the odd man out. It ripped my heart apart that they didn't want me to be present but I understood why. What hurt even more was sometime later, Henry came to my law office. He told me Lillian had given birth to not just one child, but two; she had twins. They named their baby girl Anna, after Lillian's mother and the little boy was named Phillip, after Henry's father. As far as the rest of the world knew, they were Wilcox's.

Charles said, "From that day forward, I had to pretend the twins were just my dear friends' offspring and not mine. I thought of my gift to them as my greatest accomplishment of my life as well as my greatest regret. There were times I wanted to tell Anna and Phillip that I was most likely their father, especially after their parents were killed in the car accident shortly after Phillip graduated from college. However, I am a man of my word and I kept those words to myself. Miss Pierre, no one knows this information, except for you."

I was dumbfounded by what Charles just told me. It was not my place to judge but I admit this was something I had a difficult time comprehending. I never heard of such a twist on adultery. But then again, what happened in Phillip's life was a twist on incest and my own life involved a twist on rape. Perhaps twists are necessary to get things back on track and moving forward.

I became yet another confessor, this time to Charles Watkins. In thinking about the convoluted situation, it would not make sense for me to tell Anna any of this. It was none of my business. However, before leaving the law office, I said, "Charles, I realize you never wanted anyone, especially Anna and Phillip to know you were most likely their father. However, with Phillip and your wife being gone and only Anna left, you may want to rethink your promised word of nondisclosure. If Anna were to know she is actually your child, it may open up an entirely different world for the both of you. Sometimes secrets are meant to be kept, other times, they can't help but be broken."

Within a few minutes of Charles and I finishing our conversation, Anna was back to pick me up. Charles walked me to the door and we shook hands. No other words were uttered.

Anna dropped me back off at the grape farm. I thanked her for taking me and told her that Charles and I had a good conversation. She didn't press me for any information on what we discussed and I was so very grateful for that. With that behind me, I could focus on what was important to me – Gene.

TONIGHT'S THE NIGHT

The days I spent with Gene at the grape farm were simple, yet wonderful. Every morning we would go for a long walk around the vineyard. Since it was harvesting season, Gene had to work most days. However, he still found the time to check on me in the afternoons and we had the evenings to have dinner with each other. Since Gene knew I didn't enjoy cooking, he said he would gladly do all of the cooking as long as I was willing to do the dishes with him afterward. For me, that was a small price to pay!

I was having a marvelous time. Anna and Peter brought baby Pierre and Philip to the grape farm a couple of times so I could play with them. Although it made me happy to be able to do that, at the same time it brought sadness. All I kept thinking was that I missed out on those types of opportunities with my son and granddaughter. It made me realize it was time to go back home to NOLA and my family. However, I was torn to think of leaving Gene.

Close to the end of the week, Anna, Peter, Gene and I went to the Naples Hotel for our last meal together. Terry had a special table set for us. The meal was outstanding. Kelly, John, Noah and Ella joined us for dessert. I was also surprised to see Charles Watkins come to our table and join us. Not a word was said about our conversation earlier that week. I believe he trusted me to keep his secret and I meant it when I told him I would.

The entire evening was amazing beyond words. I truly felt loved by all the new people I met in Naples. It was getting late so we said goodbye. Anna and Peter went to their home in Geneva and Gene drove us back to the grape farm. While were sitting at the kitchen table having a nightcap, he leaned over and kissed me. We both stood up and embraced each other. A very romantic, lingering kiss happened between us and I felt my heart begin to thaw. He pulled back and apologized if he was out of line.

I stepped towards him and brought him back into my arms. We shared another long, lasting kiss before he said he needed to get to bed since he had to be up early in the morning to tend to the vineyard. I was very disappointed that the evening's activities would be coming to an end and not progress to a more intimate level. I believe Gene could sense my slight agitation and he said, "Tomorrow evening is going to be our night."

The following day was spent getting all of my belongings together. At lunchtime, Gene and I took our last walk around the vineyard. I wanted to have the smell of the grapes in my mind and the taste of them on my lips. It was a bittersweet walk as we both knew our time together would be coming to an end. My train back to NOLA wasn't leaving until mid-afternoon the following day, so we would at least have some time together in the morning. Gene already worked it out with Anna that he would take me to the train station.

Anna and Peter stopped over with the twins. The word goodbye was not spoken between us. Instead, we agreed to keep in touch; forever. I told them that although there were no plans for our being together again, I knew we would be.

Gene made us a light supper that evening. After we ate, he said, "I told you yesterday that tonight is our night, Pierre." We moved the furniture to the sides of the parlor.

He turned on his phonograph record player and put on music for us to dance to. The anticipation of this evening had been with me since our first dance at the Jazz Jam. I let Gene do all the leading that night as we danced. It was wonderful to be wrapped up in this man's arms. From physically working on farms for so many years, he had a strong, sturdy body. The feelings running through my mind and body were so unusual for me. I wasn't sure what to do next. Thankfully, Gene broke the silence when he said, "There is something I wanted to ask you to do for me for quite a while." I started to think about how close we have gotten over the past two weeks. Even though we didn't know each other very well, what I thought he was going to ask me to do would be a natural progression in our relationship. But I was disappointed that it wasn't being done in the romantic way I had fantasized about; I thought it would just happen. He saw I was having deliberations and quickly blurted out, "What I want to ask you to do for me is sing "Lace Around the Moon.""

I couldn't help but burst out laughing. I told him that was not what I thought he was going to ask me to do. It was my turn to take the lead. I took his hand and said, "Gene, I would love to sing "Lace Around the Moon" for you sometime. However, that will have to wait. I am going to go to my room and get ready for bed. The door will be open and I hope you join me there."

Gene followed me into my room. From that night on, Gene and I were united in body and soul and my heart was completely thawed; I was unfrozen. I experienced intimacy I didn't know was possible and had only read about in books. Love is such a beautiful gift. Before closing our eyes for the night, I sang a few verses from "Lace Around the Moon" for him. We then drifted off to sleep.

When I woke up early in the morning, Gene was not in my bed, which I found disappointing. However, the smell of the coffee and bacon frying was just what I needed to get up and get going. I bathed and dressed for the day. When I went out to the kitchen, he was busy putting together a bag of food. He didn't see me standing there looking at him. My mind, heart, body and soul were all wrapped up in this man. I went over to him as I desperately needed to be entwined in his arms. Over breakfast, he told me that this past week had been the best week of his life. I told him I felt the same way. We agreed that we would write to each other as we didn't want what we have to end, although neither of us knew what it was we even had. No other promises were made. This way, no promises would need to be broken. We shared a passionate kiss that will forever stay on my mind, and the heart flutters that kiss brought on would forever stay in my body.

Gene brought my luggage to his auto and we drove

to the train station. After we arrived, I had a bit of a wait before the train would be taking off. Gene said he would like to stay with me until it left. However, I told him I knew he needed to be tending to the farm and I didn't want to prolong the dread of having to say goodbye to him. We kissed and I went up the steps of the train. After I turned around to look at him, I said, "Gene, please look up to the moon every night and remember that whenever you see the lace around the moon, know that our hearts will be together soon, with this, we will never be apart." I then went to my seat in the little compartment on the train. My solace was knowing it was time to go back home to my people. But I remembered thinking that I felt like the farm was becoming my second home.

TAKING CARE OF BUSINESS

On the long train ride back to NOLA, I again found myself having unfinished business, and this time it was back in NOLA. Since I would have many hours of time on my hands, I took out a pencil and a piece of paper and wrote down a list of all the things I would need to do when I got back home. My first order of business would be to invite Johnny, Tee and Maria to move in with me. Since Li'l M moved out, I admit I was lonely. I yearned to have my people with me, all of the time.

Going to my bank was another item on my list of things to do. I wanted to square away some financial matters and speak to the bank manager about who could help me get the deed to my house changed over to Johnny and Tee. It was important to me that they would know the security of home ownership.

I also wanted to go to Maria's school and ask to speak to the principal. My thought was to offer to have a small performance at her school. If Johnny and Tee agreed to this, I believe it would be a way to use music to bring Maria together with her classmates. Of course, I would make sure that Maria was comfortable with it.

There were a few other things I needed to address in due time. One of them was going to see my estranged friend, Flordie. I was not looking forward to that, I was dreading it. When I found out she had been TCA's mistress for years and the two of them orchestrated bringing the YP's to me many years ago, it was too much for me to deal with at the time. So, I told her I would contact her if and when I was ready. I was getting closer to that point, but I just wasn't there yet.

The last remaining item I would be working on was to go and visit a woman named Miss Loretta, over in Algiers Point. She held the key to so many unanswered questions I had about Frankie and D. I realized I may not like the information she could provide me with. However, never knowing the truth was harder for me to accept than being upset by it.

It was a tedious, exhausting train ride back home to NOLA. When I arrived at the train station, I was overjoyed to see Greg, Johnny, Tee and Maria waiting for me. We all embraced each other and sat down for a few minutes to get caught up on things. Johnny explained he and Tee were performing that evening at a local club so they had to leave to get ready for their show. Tee said they would like to come over and visit me in a couple of days. They surmised I would need a day to get through my mail and tend to personal matters before I would be up for visitors. I told them that sounded wonderful and I looked forward to spending some time with the three of them. They all kissed me goodbye and were on their way. Greg said he would like to give me a ride home; I enthusiastically accepted his generous offer.

When I got to my home, Greg brought in my luggage for me. We picked up all the mail that had been put under the door and placed it on my table. Greg could see how drained I was so he said he would get with me in a couple of days to discuss the new additions he was working on for the follow-up to the original "Perseverance of Pierre" articles. We said goodnight to each other and Greg left. I washed up and went to bed. I would deal with everything the following day. But for that night, I wanted to just sleep in my own bed and think about my Gene.

The following week was very busy taking care of the items on my to-do list. However, I was missing Gene terribly; he was always on my mind. But I had to put those feelings aside and get my family and personal matters taken care of. I discussed with Johnny and Tee about them moving in with me. Tee smiled and nodded affirmatively. It took Johnny a minute before he could even respond. He said, "Mother, we couldn't think of a more amazing way for all of us to get to know each other and share our lives. Since you are making this offer, we know you have thought it through and it is what you want. Therefore, we are overjoyed. We will all be a family going forward." I told them I thought if they moved in with me in early spring, that would give all of us plenty of time to get things squared away. Both of them said that would be fantastic and they couldn't wait to get home to tell Maria about all of us living together.

They seemed so excited about our upcoming living arrangements, so I thought it was the perfect time to bring up my intentions of having the deed to my house transferred to them. When I told them I wanted the three of us to go to my attorney's office to start the process of putting my property in their names, the two of them just looked at me with their mouths open. There was an awkward silence and I was worried when they didn't respond. All I could do was say, "Johnny and Tee, you have made me happier than I ever thought possible. I am so fortunate you are my family. Both of you and Maria are my everything. While I plan to be on this earth for many more years, I realize I am not getting any younger. There will be a day when I am no longer with you but I want you to be taken care of when I am gone. Please believe me when I say this is as much for me as it is for you."

Johnny took my hand and said, "If that is what you

want, we will accept your generosity. Both Tee and I grew up never knowing where we came from or who we belonged to. We lived in different apartments and dwellings but never any place we could call home. But since you came into our lives, we now have the family we have been longing for and will have a home we can call our own. Saying thank you isn't enough to express our gratitude, but we are very thankful. Please believe us when we say you are our everything as well."

Since I was on a roll, I asked if they would be amenable to me going to Maria's school to ask the principal if I could have a small singing engagement there. If Maria was comfortable with this, I would ask her to sing "Christmas Dishes" with me for her classmates. But I would want it to be just Maria and me; grandmother and granddaughter. Both Johnny and Maria smiled. Tee said, "Maria will be so excited to have this special bonding event with you Pierre. She thinks you are the most amazing person she has ever met and she can't believe how blessed she is to be your granddaughter. We will run this by her and get back to you. But we are confident she will welcome this opportunity. Please put this event together in any way you deem appropriate. We trust you, your thought processes and your decisions. After all, we are family."

Over the next several weeks, it was a hectic but wonderful time for all of us, cleaning out my house in preparation for my family moving in. One afternoon, Maria came over to help me go through my closets. We came across two boxes of my Christmas dishes. There were so many emotions connected to those glass plates. They seemed to have a life of their own. Although they were not the actual dishes that my mother and I would use to set our holiday table, they were the exact same pattern. I was fortunate to find them many years ago at a fine China shop on Royal Street. They connected me to my mother. We washed all of the dishes and put them back in their boxes. It was then that I decided we would use the dishes for our first Christmas dinner together, and God willing every Christmas after that.

Later that day after Maria left, my mail arrived and I saw there was a letter in there from Gene! My heart was racing as I quickly opened the envelope. He filled me in on how things were going at the grape farm and asked me how my trip back home went. It wasn't a long letter, but I was just so happy that he communicated with me. He ended his writing with, "Pierre, every night I go outside and look for the moon. Since there were still some leaves on the trees, I actually can see how they do look like lace! You are in my heart, Gene."

Gene's letter gave me an emotional lift and I spent the rest of the day going through my clothes, deciding which ones I would donate to the Ursuline Convent. Just when

I thought the day couldn't get better, Maria came running into my house. She came up to me, put her head on my shoulder and said, "Gran Pierre, there is nothing I would love more than our singing together at my school, except for maybe grape pie!"

JEWELS

While plugging along with my to-do items, I decided it was time to go and meet with Miss Loretta at the Jewels Supper Club in Algiers Point. I wanted to hear all she had to tell me. When Greg was working on the articles about me for the *New Orleans Observer*, he found out who Miss Loretta was. He looked back into public records and found there was a bawdy house called Miss Loretta's in Black Storyville. Black Storyville was at the back end of Storyville and was the only place where black men could go for "pleasure." In Storyville, prostitution was legal dating back to 1897. However, in 1917 when the U.S. was becoming involved in World War I, the Secretary of War did not want the troops to have distractions while deployed to NOLA. Since there were many troops stationed in the city, the U.S. Navy forced the city to shut it down and prostitution again became illegal. And since Storyville had been closed down for almost 20 years, it took Greg some digging to find out exactly who this person was. It turns out she was a petite, red-headed woman, who was previously a "comfort woman" before becoming the saloon owner of her namesake. People who misjudged her small stature and tried to cause chaos in her establishment were quickly met with a switchblade knife that she kept in her ample bosom. Patrons quickly learned not to mess with Miss Loretta if they wanted to keep their parts intact.

She also had a reputation as a savvy business owner. She was willing to open up shop in an area that lacked the grandeur of some of the houses in Storyville. She catered to the castoff clientele and became known as Loving Loretta, but she was nicknamed Double L. She accepted those who were not able to walk through the white area of Storyville into her saloon and treated everyone who entered her establishment with the respect and dignity they were not granted a few streets up. She saw the color of money and not the color of skin. It turns out that after Storyville ended, Miss Loretta moved to Algiers Point on the West Bank of the Mississippi.

I have to admit I was a bit nervous to go over to Algiers Point to meet her. However, I felt that if I had a face-to-face with Miss Loretta, I might be able to get my questions answered regarding the key with her name on it that Greg found in Frankie Quigley's box of personal effects. Thanks to Greg's investigative work, he was able to locate Frankie's family and paid them for the contents in the box; a box with many items that were life-changing for me. And even though I had my suspicions as to what Miss Loretta might tell me, I needed her confirmation.

Since I didn't want to go there alone, I asked Greg to accompany me. He already met her and knew where her supper club, Jewels, was located. I felt having him with me would make my introduction to Miss Loretta a bit less awkward.

I took special time that afternoon to make sure I was well put together. I wore one of the green dresses that TCA bought me many years ago, and I felt good. I remember years ago my mother had told me that it is better to be looked over, than overlooked. That is exactly what I was hoping to accomplish when I made my entrance into Jewels.

We took the ferry ride over and Greg held my hand to steady me off of the ferry. Jewels was a short walk from where we disembarked. I took a deep breath and said, "Let's make the most of our trip. Whatever we find out, I hope it brings more closure. I want you to know how much I appreciate you coming here with me."

We entered and headed over to the bar area. The establishment wasn't exactly what I would call opulent, but perhaps sophisticated elegance. Various colored baubles were hanging down from beautiful chandeliers throughout the dining and bar areas. It was absolutely dazzling and only reinforced my suspicion of why Jewels became the name for Miss Loretta's gem of a place!

Jewels was a feast for the eyes as well as the senses, with all the shimmering gems suspended throughout. I couldn't help myself and reached up and touched two strands of gems. They felt like cool pieces of ice in my hands.

The smells of jambalaya and crawfish boil coming from the kitchen tantalized my taste buds. As Jewels was a supper club, I also took in the enticing aroma of steaks on the grill. My mouth started to water. I knew at that moment if things went well with my conversation with Miss Loretta, I would be treating Greg to a delicious supper that evening.

The last sensory perception I had was to hear upbeat jazz and blues being played. I looked over to see a dapper gentleman in the bar who was singing a popular tune and playing guitar. He was very good and quite a showman in a well-tailored red suit with a plume feather hat. There were many reasons why Jewels was becoming a place I could see myself visiting more than once.

I was lost in thought when the hostess said, "Hello, welcome to Jewels. Will you be dining with us this afternoon?" I collected myself and asked her if Miss Loretta was available to speak with me.

I saw a small-boned, redhead walking over to us. The

woman said, "Well low and behold, the infamous Miss Pierre has come to my establishment. Please, Miss Pierre and Mr. Baynes, join me at my table over in the corner." She and I looked each other over. To me, I felt like I was sizing up an opponent. I don't know why I felt that way since I had no idea what this woman was all about. Miss Loretta was polite enough to ask us if we would like a drink. Greg and I both accepted her offer for a whiskey – neat. I was surprised when she said, "I don't see the need to make small talk with you. You are obviously here to discuss matters that involve both of us. Mr. Baynes, I don't mean to be rude, but those matters don't concern you. After the drinks are served, I am going to have my husband show you around our restaurant and entertain you until Miss Pierre and I are done talking." The three of us just sat there not even speaking. Greg and I didn't know what to say.

Thankfully our drinks arrived quickly. The man in the red suit who had been playing the guitar walked over to our table. Miss Loretta said, "I want to introduce you to my husband, Rooster." The man shook Greg's hand and said, "I am pleased to meet you both. Miss Pierre, I have followed your singing career for many years. If I may be so bold, I want you to know that I love thick-legged women." I was a bit surprised by his comment. To be honest, I was flattered. I said to Rooster, "Thank you for the compliment and for following my singing career. You are a very good singer yourself." Miss Loretta asked Rooster if he would take Greg and show him around. She said she had things she needed to discuss with me. Both Greg and Rooster excused themselves and Miss Loretta and I got down to business.

I said to Miss Loretta, "I believe we are both women who like to get to the point and I don't want to waste each other's time." I pulled out the key Greg had given me, placed it on the table, and said, "Just exactly how did you know my dear friend Frankie? I think I know the answer, but I would prefer you to tell me. I know you are under no obligation to do so, but you told Greg when you first met him that if I wanted to know things about the key and Frankie, I would have to come and speak to you myself; you would only be willing to unlock the truth to me. Well, here I am, please unlock your truth."

Miss Loretta did not even flinch when I requested this information. She took a deep breath and said, "I have wanted to get this off my chest for many years. I'm surprised it took you this long to come to me Miss Pierre. Only a few people know what I am about to tell you. Two of them have passed and with my having total trust in my husband, you would be my only liability. I read the articles in the *New Orleans Observer* about your life. So, I know some of your background. Those articles put you in a favorable light. I have a feeling some seedy details didn't make the papers, and for good reason. I have my suspicions about you and your connection to a man named Damas DuMonde."

I couldn't help but gasp when I heard my stepfather's name brought up. My mind went back to the ravagings he inflicted upon me when I was 13 years old. I took a moment to gather my thoughts on what to say next. With Miss Loretta opening the door I said, "Perhaps you will feel better about sharing your story if you first know some sordid information about me. That way, you won't feel you are the only one with something to lose." I took a deep sip of my whiskey and said, "My son Johnny is the son of Damas DuMonde. For many years I wanted to destroy that man's reputation for what he did to me. But even after I learned he was dead, I still couldn't risk people knowing of my association with him. That would have shed light on my early life, which I have gone to great lengths to keep secret, and still want to. I never want my son to know who his father was or how he came to be my son. There it is, I have laid all my cards on the table. The only people still living who knew that DuMonde was Johnny's father, and would be able to do something with that information, were Greg, my friends Flordie and Anna and now you. The way I see it, you now have something over me. I would like us to walk away this afternoon with both of us knowing we have each other's secret that we will take to our graves."

Miss Loretta dropped her head for a few seconds. It looked like she might have been saying a prayer, and then said, "Miss Pierre, I believe you are being honest with me. You're the one who has come to me and I see it in your demeanor and hear it in your words that you truly love your son, Johnny. Unfortunately, I was never able to have children but I imagine if I did, I would want to protect them the same way you are with your son. I don't see what you would have to gain now by going to the authorities about an incident that happened many years ago. I'm just having a hard time bringing myself to say the words I think you want to hear." We sat in silence for a minute. I said, "Let me be your voice. I will say what I think happened without you having to utter the words. Is that acceptable to you?" Miss Loretta looked at me and nodded her head.

Continuing, I said, "Many years ago, I believe you knew my friend, Lil' M. When she was a young woman, she was severely beaten and raped. As a result, she was crippled. I speculate this was done to her by Damas DuMonde. Not long after that, he was killed at a bawdy house he frequented. The police said it was an accident. Supposedly, a chandelier fell onto the bed where he had just been pleasured by a young girl who left the room to get soap and water to clean him up after their tryst.

Miss Loretta, I believe you were that young girl." Miss Loretta nodded her head. I went on and told her that after DuMonde would rape me when I was a young girl, he would give me a piece of beautiful jewelry. He did the same after he raped Li'l M. Therefore, I speculate the night he had his accident, he had jewels with him. When you left the room, someone else came in and was somehow able to get the chandelier to come down onto DuMonde and kill him. I believe that someone was Frankie."

Miss Loretta again nodded her head. But then her words started to flow. She said, "I truly did love Frankie. He never judged me for the line of work I was in or made me feel like a whore. Up until meeting him, I never thought I would be anything else. He changed my life and I believe he truly loved me. After the incident with DuMonde, we saw it as a way out of our hard lives. It would be our fresh start. However, we couldn't risk selling the jewels until the dust had cleared with DuMonde's death. Frankie and I scraped together all of our money to open a saloon in Black Storyville. We didn't have enough, until one day, Frankie told me we had all the money we would need. I never questioned him. I figured the less I knew, the better. To me, it didn't matter where the money came from. What mattered was we were able to open up Miss Loretta's and I no longer had to service men on my back. I would be servicing them standing upright, pouring them a drink.

However, all my hopes and dreams for the future came crashing down when Frankie died in the roofing accident. I at least had the jewels to fall back on. A few months after Frankie's passing, I took a trip to New York City and was able to sell them. With the money from the sale, I eventually invested in Jewels.

I told Miss Loretta I felt for her after having lost Frankie. But there was one question I had that I would appreciate her answering. I asked her what the key with the name "Miss Loretta's" on it had to do with all of this. She said, "There is no mystery to that; it was Frankie's key to our place, Miss Loretta's in Black Storyville. I lived in the back apartment of the property and my name was on the deed as the owner. That ensured there was no way to legally connect Frankie to "Miss Loretta's." Frankie was always there doing things around the building. He was very good with woodworking and he made a small, secret compartment in the bottom of the wood area of the bar. That is where we hid the jewels. When it came time for me to name this establishment, Jewels was the most profound name I could think of. A strange series of events led to my having Jewels. I believe what goes around comes around Miss Pierre."

Miss Loretta downed her drink and asked the server for a bottle of champagne to be brought to the table. She confirmed that my suspicions were accurate for the most part. However, there was something that was left out. I did not see it coming when she said, "Frankie may have been the brawn behind DuMonde's demise. However, it was Timothy C. Anderson who orchestrated it. Frankie told me Anderson wanted DuMonde to pay for what he did to you when you were a young girl. He also said Anderson was in love with you; you were his angel."

I didn't even have time to comprehend what she just told me as the server arrived with the bottle of expensive champagne. Miss Loretta said it was a bottle she had been saving for a special occasion. She asked that the champagne be poured into two crystal flutes that were also brought to us. Miss Loretta asked me to join her in a toast. She raised her glass and said, "To *liberté* – our freedom and to Frankie!"

Miss Loretta got up from her seat and said she was going to go find Rooster and Greg and ask them to share the champagne with us. I asked her if we could stay for dinner and if she and Rooster would like to join us. She said, "Of course you can stay and have dinner, but it will be my treat. However, today's meeting has been rough on my heart and soul. I need to decompress and go upstairs with Rooster to our apartment."

The four of us finished off the bottle of champagne. Miss Loretta and Rooster said they were calling it a night. We all got up from the table and surprisingly, Miss Loretta hugged me! Rooster shook Greg's hand and gave me a hug and a wink. He then said, "I am glad I have had the opportunity to meet you and your thick legs." Greg and I watched the two of them walk away as the server came back over to our table. I said, "Greg, we are going to have an awesome steak dinner on Miss Loretta!"

What a fantastic dinner it was! I wouldn't say Miss Loretta and I parted as friends, however, we did part as comrades. Perhaps friendship would one day come. True to Miss Loretta's word, there was no charge for our dinner. Greg and I left to go back to the ferry. While we were sitting there, he asked me if everything was all right. I told him I had a sense of closure after meeting with Miss Loretta. The doors that had been swinging open for many years were shut. Perhaps new doors could then be opened.

Greg saw me back to my house. I thanked him for all he had done for me, putting my life on track and making it possible for me to move forward with my family. We hugged each other and I stepped back from him. I started to cry and told him not to worry about me. My tears were not tears of sorrow but of contentment. I composed myself and said, "Greg, I am blessed to have you as my second son and I love you." As I walked inside, I wasn't the only one who was wiping away tears.

That evening I sat outside in my little courtyard. I was able to breathe a sigh of relief that I had taken care of most of the items I wanted to since returning to NOLA. There was still the matter of contacting Flordie. I was working on that, but I still wasn't ready.

SECURE LOVE

Gene and I continued our letter-writing relationship; how I looked forward to his letters. They were not overly romantic, but then again, neither was he. But I could tell what he was saying in his letters was from his heart. He wrote it outright in one of them–

"Pierre, every morning when I wake up and then when I am out working in the fields, you are on my mind. By lunchtime, I am parched and hungry. I reflect on the times we shared wine and food and you are again on my mind. Then when it is time for me to go to sleep, I remember you singing a few verses from your song and how your body felt when I touched you with my weathered farmer's hands. Let me just say you are always on my mind and in my heart. I am falling in secure love with you."

That letter contained the most heartfelt words ever shared with me. It made me feel like I was adored. I quickly wrote back to Gene and told him I too was having deep feelings for him. However, I wrote that I didn't understand exactly what "secure love" was.

About two weeks went by and I didn't receive a letter. I was a bit disappointed but also nervous that perhaps his feelings changed or maybe I upset him by asking what he meant by "secure love". My insecurities dissipated one afternoon when Greg asked me to come to the *New Orleans Observer* to look over the draft he prepared for the next installation of the articles on the "Perseverance of Pierre." When I arrived, he took me over to a room that had what looked like a telegraph, some other electronic equipment and a telephone. Greg got right to the point. He said he worked it out with Michele back in Naples for him to place a call to the *Naples Newspaper* where Gene would be waiting for our call. I was flabbergasted this was happening! Gene did not have a telephone at the grape farm. The one that was previously there was taken out after Phillip went to jail and I did not yet have one in my house. So, it never occurred to me to have a telephone conversation with him. Greg saw the look of confusion on my face. He put me at ease when he said, "Pierre, just talk to Gene from your heart, the words will come." He asked if I was ready for him to place the call. All I could do was shake my head affirmatively. It took about 10 minutes before we were finally able to be connected. Greg then walked away so I could talk in private.

When I heard Gene's voice through the telephone line, I had to catch my breath. The connection wasn't the best but I could hear Gene say, "Is that you, Pierre?" I responded, "Yes, Gene it is me, and I am overwhelmed with how amazing it is that Greg and Michele set this up for us! I don't want to talk for too long as I am sure this is an expense for them and I don't want to take advantage of their generosity." Gene asked how everything was going. I told him all was well and I asked him about himself and Anna and her family. He confirmed they were all fine.

With the pleasantries out of the way, I asked him what he meant in his last letter where he said he was falling in "secure love" with me. Gene said, "Most of us are fortunate to fall in love. That is what keeps the world going. However, I have found that as we get older, what you want or expect out of love changes. Of course, the optimal situation would be to spend every day with the one you love. But if that is not possible, you still can be in love. It just changes the dynamics. I have been thinking a great deal about what you and I have between us, Pierre. The best way I can define how I feel about you is what I call secure love. The word secure means to be fastened, as not to give way, become loose or be lost; I think that is what we have." Before I could even respond, Gene said, "If you are up for a visit from me, I would love to come and spend about a week with you in your precious city. I want to really get to know both of you!" My response was an enthusiastic, "Yes please!" Gene said that he had talked with Michele and she too wanted to come to NOLA to see Greg. Michele was able to convince the editor of the *Naples Newspaper*, Destiny, to pay for her trip. The newspaper recognized that Michele was collaborating with Greg to promote the connection between the two cities. While in NOLA, she would be working on a follow-up to the article she had previously published in the *Naples Newspaper*.

He and Michele would work out their travel arrangements. They were planning to come towards the middle of January, after the holidays. Gene said, "I will write you as soon as we have everything finalized. I securely love you, Pierre." My heart was fluttering and I went to respond to him that I too was securely in love with him, however, before I could complete the sentence, the phone line went dead and we were disconnected.

As I hung up the telephone, my heart was fluttering and beating so fast. Although I was disappointed that Gene didn't get to hear me say how I also securely loved him, I was glad I would have the opportunity when he came to visit me!

Greg came back into the room. He hugged me and said he was so glad Michele and Gene would be coming to NOLA. After that embrace, he got down to business. He had the final draft of the articles that would be published in the *New Orleans Observer* ready for me to look over. Playfully, I scolded Greg for setting up the call with Gene without my knowing about it. But I then said, "Greg you never cease to amaze me. Since I met you, my life keeps getting better and better. Without you, the person you see before you would not exist. I don't know how to properly thank you, but I will find a way."

On my way out of Greg's office, he put the draft entitled, "The Perseverance of Pierre – Her Journey Forward," into a bag for me. He explained it would run for two consecutive Sundays once it had been finalized and asked if I could please have the draft back to him in a week.

When I arrived home, I took the draft out to my little courtyard where I spent the remainder of the afternoon making small editorial notes. Overall, Greg and Michele did an outstanding job! It made me proud of my perseverance and how it was portrayed in the articles. I returned the draft to Greg the very next day. Within two weeks, the first article ran in the *New Orleans Observer*. After that, I couldn't believe how my popularity grew even greater. My people, the people of NOLA, embraced me and I was honored that I did them proud!

ROSE COLORED GLASSES

True to his word, I received a letter from Gene a week later and eagerly opened the envelope with a smile on my face. In it were the specifics with the date, estimated time of arrival and the ticket number.

With this information, I started to prepare for Gene's visit. Spending time with him was all I could think about. It made me realize that love is for all ages. Although my body was not able to carry me as it did as a young woman, my heart didn't have any idea how old my body was. All I knew was that my heart was wrapped up in a farmer from Naples, NY. Secure love was changing my life and healing my body and soul.

There was only one thing I worried about that could derail the wonderful time I anticipated Gene and I having; miscegenation laws which enforce racial segregation at the level of marriage and intimate relationships. Since Gene had never been to the South before, he wouldn't know about how divided things were in NOLA. Although our politicians would say that racial segregation is constitutional as long as the facilities and services provided for blacks and whites were roughly equal – that was not the case. It was not what I was living. Although I was able to go into some "white-only" places to perform, it still bothered me deeply that I was only allowed in because of my respected singing career.

In my last letter to Gene before his arrival, I had to spell it out for him that although he didn't have any issues with my being a black woman, the rest of the South did. I worried our racially segregated worlds would collide. Gene and I never really discussed the fact that he was white and I was black. It didn't matter to us. But I didn't want Gene to be unaware of what he might encounter when he was in the city I loved, but sometimes didn't understand.

In my letter, I clarified that after the Reconstruction era, racial segregation in the American South was enforced through Jim Crow laws. These laws were widespread and aimed at oppressing the black population in the South. Jim Crow was not an actual person, but rather a fictional minstrel character developed and popularized by Thomas Rice. He would perform his song and dance act in blackface and supposedly his character was modeled after a slave. Jim Crow became kind of a shorthand for the statutes and ordinances that segregated and demeaned African Americans; that segregated and demeaned me. Even more insulting was the implementation of the legal doctrine under U.S. Constitutional law called "separate but equal." As a result of those laws and policies, I had to use different water fountains, restrooms, hospitals, theatres, hotels and restaurants than white people. Even our schools were segregated; Maria had to go to a "colored-only" school. With those doctrines, blacks have received inferior treatment. We were not treated as equals and I didn't see this disparity or oppression coming to an end anytime soon, at least not in my lifetime. I ended my letter to Gene telling him I have had to adapt to this derogatory oppression all of my adult life. However, it broke my heart when I tried to explain all of this to Maria. There simply were no words that could make it right for her or any other black child in the South.

Much to my surprise and delight I received a telegram from Gene, rather than a letter. It was very brief - "I received your letter explaining how things are so racially divided where you live. Although geography is one of the obstacles in our relationship, I now understand the color of our skin is another one. I have taken off my rose-colored glasses and realize we are not going to be able to change the unfair practices that are in place. However, our relationship goes beyond color barriers. I am looking forward to spending time with you in New Orleans, no matter what barriers we may encounter. I securely love you."

BIENVENUE – WELCOME!

I couldn't let my insecurities overshadow my anticipation of Gene's arrival. It was surreal to me that Gene was coming all this way to be with me. For over two months, I had been anxiously awaiting Gene's visit and I was very glad that he and Michele were traveling together. Greg was having the same feelings, as he too was excited for Michele's visit to NOLA. During the time Greg and I were waiting for our special people to come to us, we bonded even more. It was great for both of us to talk about our new loves and the plans we were making for them while they were with us, in our city!

Knowing that Greg and I would want to have private time with our loves, we made a plan. He would drop Gene and me off at my house after picking our people up from the train station. Then, over the next couple of days, each couple would spend time on their own. However, we would all meet for dinner later in the week.

Gene's arrival date finally came. Greg picked me up in his automobile and we went to the train station. I wore a simple dress and jewelry; I didn't want to overdo anything on Gene's initial steps into NOLA. I wanted to ease him into my fold. When I saw Gene exit the train, my heart fluttered. He was looking for me and when our eyes connected, the flutter happened again. Those flutters I kept having were amazing feelings and not easy to come by. Yes, I was falling in love with this man.

After I hugged and kissed Gene, I looked over to Greg and Michele and noticed the same looks of love on their faces. This was going to be a life-changing week for the four of us; I just felt it. We all made small talk on the ride to my house. Gene asked if he could take me out to dinner somewhere close to where I lived, as he knew I didn't much care for cooking. Laughingly I said, "Thank you for being astute to my lack of culinary skills, however, while I can't cook, I have friends who can. There is a meal waiting for us when we get back to my place."

Watching Gene and Michele's reactions to our plants and tree foliage, the structure of the streets, the different style homes and buildings we passed by on our ride was priceless. Their mouths were open in awe of the Crescent City! Michele commented that the color of the landscape back in New York was mostly white with the snow. But here in NOLA, she couldn't believe there was greenery and flowers in bloom! Gene chimed in on how interesting the architecture of the buildings was. Greg explained to him that a great many of the structures were Creole style, which represented a melding of the French, Spanish and Caribbean architectural influences. He also explained the houses in many of the neighborhoods were referred to as "shotgun" houses. All rooms are in a direct line with each other, usually front to back. If a bullet was shot from the front door, it would pass through the house without hitting anything and would exit through the back door.

We pulled up to my little home and Gene said he was delighted to see that I lived in a shotgun house! He couldn't wait to see what the inside looked like. I thanked Greg for picking Gene up and dropping us off. We confirmed our plans for later in the week when we would be going to dinner at Antone's, a well-established Creole restaurant in the French Quarter. Hugs were exchanged and I said to Michele, "Hopefully you and Greg will have a wonderful evening. You are in good hands with this man. There is no doubt he will take you to many wonderful places NOLA has for you to experience. My hope is at the end of the visit you love our city as much as we do. *Laissez les bon temps rouler!*"

When Gene and I were finally alone, he gently brought me to his body using his brawny arms and kissed me deeply. When we separated from the lingering kiss, I asked him if he would like a drink. He said he brought some of his wine with him and asked if I would like to have that with our dinner. Gene went into his luggage and pulled out the wine along with a large bag of grapes! I asked him why he brought so many grapes and he explained he wanted to bake a grape pie for Maria and my family. To me, that gesture spoke right to my heart and tastebuds!

We enjoyed a glass of wine together, talking about his train trip. He said he was savoring the experience. After we finished our wine, we went into my little kitchen and ate the muffuletta sandwich I picked up earlier in the day from my favorite local market. Gene marveled at the taste and textures of this huge sandwich. I explained to him that the base was Italian sesame bread. The spread on the sandwich is made of olive salad with layers of mortadella, salami, ham, Swiss and provolone cheese. The muffuletta was a meal in itself; we were not able to finish it. Gene said it was the best sandwich he ever had! He planned to take the recipe back to Naples and suggest that the Arnos try it out on their menu.

Although the muffuletta was very filling, I thought Gene might welcome something sweet to eat after our meal. Therefore, I also picked up bread pudding for dessert. It was on the counter and I started to plate it. Gene said he was exhausted from his trip and would love to wait and have it in the morning. I asked him if he was up for a nightcap. He said he would love a whiskey - neat. We chatted for a bit and finished our drinks. I then took Gene's hand and brought him to my bed. On that special night in my bedroom, Jim Crow laws didn't apply. Although I was a black woman from the South, to Gene, I was just a woman – his woman. After that night, I wasn't falling in love with this man, I was in love with him!

EXPLORATION

We woke up early in the morning and made coffee to have with our bread pudding. Gene looked refreshed from the previous day's journey. I put out clean water and soap so we could wash up and get dressed. We sat there at my table having our simple breakfast, both of us so happy to be together. Since we were in my city, I asked him if he was comfortable with me planning our days while he was here. He said, "I would very much welcome that since I have no idea where to even begin to make the days special for us. Please take the lead! However, there is only one thing I would request we do while I am here with you. If it is possible, I would like for all of us to have a communal supper that we could prepare together and share before I go back to New York. I would like to bake a grape and apple pie for dessert for the meal."

I told Gene I thought that was a fantastic idea. However, my little house would not be able to accommodate all of the people who I thought we should invite. Quickly thinking over the special supper, it occurred to me that we could have it at *Liberté*. There would be plenty of room there to set up a table for about 10 people. Since I had already planned for us to go to *Liberté* to meet Li'l M and see Tee, it would be the perfect time to set up our family/ friends' supper. Even though I recently sold my share of *Liberté* to Lil'M and Tee, I still felt a strong connection to the business and wanted Gene to see it.

After breakfast, we walked over there. When we arrived, Tee and Maria embraced Gene as if he were one of their own. He was genuinely happy to see them and I think he felt love from my family. Lil' M went right up to him and hugged him! She stepped back from him and said, "I have never seen my dear friend Pierre as happy and content as she is now in her life. She has always been considered to be the gem of NOLA. However, now because of you, she is a sparkling gem."

We showed Gene around *Liberté*. He said he was impressed with the essence of NOLA that he felt at our establishment. We were all talking when we heard a knock at the door. Lil' M answered it and brought Flordie into the parlor area. Unbeknownst to me, Lil' M had contacted her and asked her to come by when she found out Gene and I would be coming to *Liberté* for a visit. Just as many years ago when Flordie came to *Liberté* and Lil' M and I welcomed her into our hearts, I did the same that day. Although I had been estranged from Flordie due to circumstances regarding TCA, I let it all go.

All of us sat down for some coffee and homemade sweets Flordie brought with her from her bakery. I explained to Lil' M, Tee and Flordie that Gene and I would like to have a supper at *Liberté* for all of us. Lil'M excitedly said, "That would be divine! Flordie joined in and said she would like to do some of the cooking and Tee said she and Johnny could do all the setup. Gene volunteered to get chickens that he would brine and roast. He also said he would bake Maria a grape pie. Maria started clapping and gave Gene a hug of gratefulness. I was amazed at the magnanimity of this group. Within a couple of minutes of saying we would like to have a dinner – it was all figured out! We all came up with the menu and Gene and I were on our way.

Our first stop was the butcher shop where we put in an order for several fresh chickens. I knew the owner and he said he would have them prepared for us the following day and would even drop them off at my house. From there, we headed over to the French Market for other items Gene would need to prepare the chicken dish and the pies. He was definitely in his element shopping at the French Market. There were so many spices and foods he had never seen before. Gene was like a child in a candy store! We spent a few hours there. Although it would not have been a wise idea for Gene to hold my hand and draw attention to ourselves, he would slightly brush my arm or stand close enough to me that I could feel his body against mine. Those small gestures endeared him to me even more and at the same time stimulated some of my senses.

It was getting late and we were both tired. We decided to pick up some food that we could eat back at my home. Once we arrived, food was the last thing on our minds.

Again, we woke up early the following day. Before meeting Gene, I never woke at the crack of dawn. But with him, I loved experiencing the sunrise. We washed up, dressed for the day and were on our way to *Café Du Monde.* I wanted him to experience what chicory coffee and beignets tasted like. Gene enjoyed the simple breakfast there. He said he was going to try and make beignets back home in Naples so the next time I came to visit him there, I could have a taste of NOLA. I liked that he was already thinking about me going back to the grape farm. We both were on the same page; each envisioning our future together.

We walked over to St. Louis Cathedral so we could light a candle and say a prayer. Gene was not a religious man. His philosophy was "Dear God, save my soul, if I have a soul." However, he marveled at how beautiful the church was and said he was glad to experience going with me since he knew how much the church meant to me. On our way to Canal Street for clothes shopping, we walked through Jackson Square. I asked him if we could sit down for a minute on my favorite bench. While we were relaxing, I told Gene about a few of the monumental experiences that happened in my life right in Jackson Square. Gene took my hand and said, "I understand why you find solace at the Square, I feel it too. Before I go back to Naples, I would like to stop here again."

From there, we were on a mission to find Gene a dinner jacket and tie to wear for our dinner with Greg and Michele at Antone's. We went to one of the men's specialty clothing shops that I knew would welcome both of us in. When we arrived, I told him I would like to buy him the clothing he needed. At first, he was not comfortable accepting my offer, however, I explained to him that the royalties coming in from "Lace Around the Moon" were more than I ever thought possible and it would make me happy to do this for him. He graciously accepted the jacket and tie. We had the shop owner wrap the items up and we continued to our next destination.

Just up the street, we went into a small clothing boutique that my friend Rebecca Gannon and her husband Walt owned. Rebecca and I exchanged pleasantries and I introduced her to Gene. She went into the back of the shop and came out with Walt. Gene and Walt started chatting with each other and they became engrossed in conversation; it was like they were long-lost friends. Rebecca and I left them so I could look around at all the beautiful clothing on display. Out of the corner of my eye, I saw an eye-catching purple dress the color of an amethyst crystal. I asked her if they had it in my size and they did. When I came out to model it for Gene, his head turned in my direction and he abruptly stopped talking with Walt. He simply said, "Pierre you must have the dress. You look spectacular in it! And just as I accepted your generosity in purchasing my new apparel, I hope you will accept this dress from me." For the first time in many years, I had an outfit purchased for me by a man other than TCA. It was a fresh start. Everything with Gene was fresh and new. Something as simple as a new dress was life-changing and a step in the right direction. Another door had just been shut while a new one was slowly opening.

After leaving the boutique, we walked back to my house to get dressed and ready to go to the Golden Dragon where Johnny, Tee and the Lagniappe Orchestra would be performing. Gene marveled at how everything was within walking distance. Back home in Naples, he needed an automobile to get around to do shopping, postal drop-offs and just about anything. He thought NOLA was a city where things were simple, yet extraordinarily complicated at the same time.

SELF-ACTUALIZATION

When Gene and I entered the Golden Dragon, the host immediately took us over to a special table. I left Gene there and went behind the stage to talk with Johnny, Tee and the band. They were all excited for the opportunity to perform in the Astoria section of the night club which was for African-American audiences. The venue hosted performers including Louis Armstrong, so this was quite an achievement for the band. We confirmed that I would only join them on "Lace Around the Moon." It was important to me for them to bask in the glory of their accomplishments and be recognized on their own merits, not just because of their association with me. However, at the same time, I was there to support them in any way I could.

Although swing jazz was popular in New Orleans, the Lagniappe Orchestra stayed true to traditional jazz music and they performed flawlessly. They truly were captivating and the crowd connected with them on every song Johnny and the band played and that Tee sang. I was in awe of their stage performance. They were on par with many of the well-known jazz bands playing throughout the Quarter. Honestly, they were even better. I realized I may have been preferential in my opinion. However, with my being in the business for many years, I felt I could offer up that sincere assessment.

The band had one more song to perform before intermission, followed by a short break before the second half of the show. That was when Jeremy, our band leader, introduced me and asked me to come to the front and join them. The crowd went wild with applause when I went onto the stage. The band and I performed "Lace Around the Moon." The audience was silent while I sang but then erupted into cheers at the end of the song. After we finished, the accolades I received were overwhelming and rewarding. I stood there suspended in time thinking back to the scared, pregnant young girl who first came to NOLA a lifetime ago. Although it took 50-plus years encountering many obstacles, heartbreaks and setbacks, I was finally in a place I never could have imagined possible. Maria Pierre Quinones was before a crowd of adoring fans who were chanting, "Pierre! Pierre!" I never really felt the magnitude of my accomplishments until that moment and I admit I was proud of myself. The highlight of that night was Gene being there in the audience staring at me with such admiration it elevated me to a height of self-actualization I never knew was achievable.

After I took a bow, Johnny guided me off of the stage and back to my table. I was a bit shaky as I sat down next to Gene. He embraced me and whispered, "Pierre, you were spellbinding!"

My head was a whirlwind of thoughts and emotions and what happened next, made my mind skip a beat. Different people came over to our table to say hello and continued to offer kind words about my performance. After a couple of minutes, three women approached us and stood before me. Before I recognized her face, I recognized her voice when she said, "Darling, are you looking for us?" Those were the exact same words this woman said to me about 50 years ago. I couldn't believe my ears and eyes! It was Dee, Irene and Erina – my CC's! I stood up and we all hugged and kissed each other as tears flowed down my face. They said they didn't want to stay too long chatting as the band's intermission was almost over. We made a plan to meet up and reconnect. I told them I was over the moon with happiness in seeing them and thanked them for coming out to support me. Oh, what a night it turned out to be!

Gene and I stayed until the end of the band's performance. I hugged Johnny, Tee and all the band members. They joined us for a drink before Gene and

I left. Sometimes gratitude and admiration cannot be expressed with just words. So, I asked all of them if we could join together for our "blessing bend." This was a ceremonial ritual we would do after a successful event. Joining arms with an elbow lock we bent our heads down for a moment of reflection. I said, "Dear God, thank you for the opportunity we were given tonight to perform in this beautiful venue. You have guided our path to this success and we are indebted. The friendships that we have developed between us are what we are most thankful for. We are blessed and we are grateful." After we were done with the prayer, we raised our heads, dropped our arms and did a knee bend.

After leaving the Golden Dragon, Gene and I walked back to my house and planned to go right to sleep since we were exhausted from the long but wonderful day. Gene surprised me and asked if we could join together in an elbow lock. After we did, he asked me to bend my head and he said, "Pierre, I am offering up a "blessing bend" of my own. The greatest blessing of my life has been meeting you." We both did a knee bend and kissed each other good night; it continued to be a very good night.

BREAKING BREAD

When Gene and I woke up on the morning of our communal supper, we were excited to start preparing for it. The day before, we arranged with Flordie that we would bring the chickens over to her bakery. She said she had room in her ovens for them to cook properly. After we were dressed, we headed over to Flordie's. When we arrived, she had coffee and sweets waiting for us. She and Gene started working on roasting the chickens and getting the pies ready for baking. I was very grateful to her for stepping up to the plate to make this dinner happen. Without her assistance, it would not have been possible.

With Gene and Flordie having things under control in her kitchen, I left them to go to the market to pick up the items we would need for the salad. It didn't take long to round up the fresh greens and other vegetables. When I returned, the two of them were up to their elbows in butter, flour, apples and grapes! It touched me to see the two of them working together and getting along so well.

Since I wasn't of much use to them in the kitchen, I told them I would be going over to *Liberté*.

Upon entering the building, the smell of roses filled the house. It wasn't until I walked into the room down the hall that I saw three large flower vases filled with pink roses! They were beautifully arranged and it made me feel so special that my people did that for me. Their kind gesture motivated me to put my special cleaning skills to use. In no time, *Liberté* was dusted and immaculate! Johnny and Maria had already set up the long table and chairs and Lil' M had laid out lovely tablecloths, napkins and silverware on the counter. Since I had time, I decided to set the table. Looking through the cupboards, I only found five plates. Using all the items Lil' M had set out, I put together a beautiful table, minus the four additional plates we would need.

Gene and I planned to meet back at my house after he finished preparing the food for our feast. With the day quickly passing, I headed back home to dress and round up plates from my cupboards to bring back to *Liberté*. After I finished getting ready, Gene returned. He was covered in even more flour and had other stains on his shirt. It didn't seem to bother him as he went to wash up and get ready. When he came out of my dressing room, he looked like a different man and was wearing an earthy scent cologne that fit his personality. I nestled my nose into his neck for just a moment and when I stepped back, he drew me in for an intoxicating kiss. He held me and said, "Pierre, I want you to know I am having a sensational time helping prepare our supper. I love to cook and break bread with people. But what I really love is that we are doing it together. Every time I think the day I spend with you couldn't get any better, it does!

After packing up a few things we needed, including the plates, we were off! When we arrived, Lil' M and Tee were also coming in with red beans and rice and the shrimp and grits Lil' M had prepared. Johnny, Maria and Flordie were not far behind them with the chickens and pies. Flordie also baked some loaves of bread to accompany our meal. There was so much food they needed to use a wagon to transport it all! Since cooking was not involved with making the salad, I gladly said I would go into the kitchen area and put it together. While I was doing that, everyone else took the food into the room where we would be eating. When I entered the room with the salad, I saw that instead of the mismatched plates I collected throughout the day being on our table, there were my beloved Christmas dishes! Seeing them on the table with all of the people that mattered to me, brought me to tears. Tee said that when they knew I would be out of my house during the day, they went there, picked them up and brought them to *Liberté*. I looked at each person individually for a brief moment; Johnny, Tee, Maria, Greg, Michele, Flordie, Lil' M and Gene and I lovingly said, "Thank you for making this one of the most special days of my life. And since these Christmas dishes remind me of my mother and mean so much to me, Maria, I would like for you to have them when you are older. I know you will cherish them as much as I do. They will be in good hands!"

When we all sat down to eat and everyone had a drink in front of them, Gene stood up and asked if he could propose a toast. We all raised our glasses and Gene said, "I am honored to be here with all of you and be part of this amazing group of family and friends. My life has changed since I met Pierre, her family and all of you. Like most people, I have gone through my life appreciative of what I have. However, until now, I didn't realize how good things could be."

Johnny asked us all to hold hands around the table and he led us in prayer. The meal from start to finish was delicious! The grape and apple pies were scrumptious. Maria even ate all of her food on her plate before eating her slice of grape pie. Of course, she asked if she could take another piece of grape pie home with her and she quickly wrapped it up!

Everyone was having a wonderful time but when we were done, we couldn't believe how much food was left over. I suggested instead of trying to pack it up and find places to keep it so it wouldn't spoil, we open our doors to the neighbors. Next door to *Liberté*, there was an herbal business that my friends, Michael and Mary Grace Corsi owned. Both of them were into holistic medicines and potions and they were well revered in our area. I went over to their store and invited them to join us. They graciously accepted our offer and came in to meet everyone and share in our meal.

Even after they finished, there was still some uneaten food we didn't want to go to waste. Mary Grace shared with us that her mother would quote a verse from Ecclesiastes with her own twist on it, "Cast your bread upon the waters and you will get cake." Although the actual verse is, "Cast your bread upon the waters, for you will find it after many days," we all told her we liked her mother's saying better! The message of both quotes was the same, we should all be generous even if a return is unlikely. The words Mary Grace shared with us were inspiring. Gene and I told everyone we would be back in 15 minutes with some people who might appreciate some pie rather than cake!

It only took us walking a block to find three vagrants who were roaming the street and looked like they would welcome a hot meal. We invited them to come with us to *Liberté*. Two of them were skeptical of our gesture, however, that didn't stop them from following us back. After we escorted them to our table, they sat down and all my people treated these men as if they were one of us. Three plates of food were quickly made up and set before them. They ate the food quickly and thanked us. Tee and Flordie packed up three separate bags of whatever food was left for each of them to take home. However, there were only two pieces of apple pie left. Amazingly, Maria took the piece of grape pie she had wrapped up to take home and brought it over to the table. She said she would like to give it to one of the men so they could each leave with a piece of pie. I could see in her parents' eyes that they too were in awe of their daughter, my granddaughter, for her selfless act of kindness. When Maria gave up her pie, that was our cake coming back to us. Maria did us proud!

After we said goodbye to the three men, Mary Grace and Michael, we all cleaned up the room and Gene and I did the dishes. Everyone was too full from dinner to even have a nightcap. Johnny and Tee said they would bring my Christmas dishes back to the house the following day. We all said goodnight to each other and Greg and I confirmed that Gene and I would be meeting him and Michele the following evening for dinner at Antone's.

On our way back home, Gene and I saw one of the men who came to our supper on the street corner. He was sharing the food we had given him with a woman and two young children. The bread we had cast that day fed several people and it felt so rewarding!

Gene and I were so exhilarated from the day's event we were not even tired or maybe we were over tired. We took a bottle of Gene's wine out to my courtyard and just talked. Since I had been living alone for quite some time since Lil' M moved out, having someone to share my days and nights with was so enjoyable. It was a feeling of security on some level and the haunting loneliness was not with me since Gene's arrival. Some people seem to handle the hollowness of desolation with ease; not me. It wasn't until I spent the past several days with Gene that I realized I didn't want to spend the rest of my life without him.

That night when Gene and I went to bed, he spooned me and held me tight. The feelings that embrace brought me were of peace and serenity; it put me to sleep like I was a baby. That was something I could get used to.

BETROTHMENT

We arrived at Antone's with both of us looking like we belonged there. Gene was so handsome in his fashionable attire and I felt spectacular in my new purple dress. When we went in, we were immediately greeted by the current owner, Ray. He had recently become the owner, taking over for his father Julius, and he couldn't have been more gracious to both of us. We explained we were early and waiting for our other guests to join us. Ray asked us if we would like to have a private tour of his establishment. We accepted his offer and went from room to room and marveled at the restaurant's sophisticated NOLA elegance and decor. He even took us to their legendary wine cellar. I think their wine cellar was another one of the highlights of Gene's trip.

When we were done, Ray brought us back to the entrance area where Greg and Michele were waiting for us. He instructed his *maître d'* to take us to our table. He started to walk us over to the main dining area. However, I told him I would prefer for us to sit in the "colored" section of the restaurant. No other words were exchanged; he gave us their best table in that area and we were treated like royalty for the entire evening. The waiter attentively came to our table and recommended Oysters Rockefeller as an appetizer for the table. Both Gene and Michele said they never had them before but were intrigued and wanted to try them. They were not disappointed. The entire meal was outstanding!

The four of us discussed the different things we had been doing over the past few days. Both Michele and Gene couldn't stop talking about how much they were enjoying their time in NOLA. Greg and I sat there listening to their conversation and just smiled at each other. We both knew we were exactly where we wanted to be and with the people we wanted to be with.

It was getting late so Greg and Michele said they would be leaving to go to a jazz club. Michele had taken to the music of our city and Greg wanted her to get as much of it as possible before she had to go back to Naples the following afternoon. We asked the *maître d'* for our bill. It was Ray who came back to our table and said, "There is no charge for you and your party Miss Pierre. What you have done for our city, cannot be repaid. Let this be my small token of appreciation. You are not just the gem of

New Orleans, you are a "cardinal gem;" a gemstone more precious than any other."

After thanking Ray for the fabulous dinner and his hospitality, we all walked to the front door to leave. I thought Gene and I would walk back to my house after seeing Michele and Greg to their auto. However, Gene said he would like to walk over to Jackson Square if I was up for it. It was a lovely evening with many stars in the night sky. We sat on my favorite bench holding hands. After a couple of minutes, Gene turned to me and said, "Pierre, the people in this city truly adore you. Everyone we have come in contact with wants to pay tribute to you in their own special way. I feel honored and humbled to be part of your life, as you are the most amazing woman I have ever met. I realize we have only been together for a short time, however, our relationship seems to be timeless to me and I am hoping you feel the same way. With that all being said, I want you to know I am somewhat of a traditional man. But what we have is not a traditional love affair. I want to spend my life with you under whatever conditions we can make happen. Until that time, I want you to have a piece of jewelry from me that is my symbol of love and commitment to you. It represents how we have come together in a continuous circle of love, even if we are not always physically together. Gene took out a small box, opened it and took out an exquisite bracelet from inside. He fastened it onto my wrist and explained how he had a jeweler put an emerald and amethyst gem into the gold chain and that the charms of grape clusters and *fleur de lis* on it represented the grape farm and NOLA.

The bracelet was extraordinary! The fact that he put so much thought into it, made it even more precious to me. Also, his choosing Jackson Square as the place to give it to me mattered a great deal.   I said to Gene, "If you have it in your heart to be with me for the rest of our lives, under whatever arrangement we can come up with, I accept this promise bracelet." Gene corrected me when he got down on one knee and said, "This is not a promise bracelet, it is an engagement bracelet. I realize we may not ever be able to go and get a marriage license and marry under normal circumstances. But that won't stop me from wanting to make it happen in our Gene-Pierre world. Just because we won't have an official piece of paper saying we are married in the eyes of the law, we will be married in our own eyes."

I was elated by Gene's words and told him I would accept his commitment of secure love represented by the gorgeous bracelet. "Yes Gene, I will marry you in our own way." We sealed our commitment to each other with an endearing kiss and walked back home arm in arm. I was over the moon!

To celebrate, we had a glass of white wine that Gene brought with him. It was the closest thing we had to champagne. He toasted us and said he looked forward to our future life together, whatever that life may be or where it might take us. I started to think I wanted to do something special for Gene the following day; our last day together before he returned to Naples. His train wasn't scheduled to leave until 5:00 pm so we would have plenty of time to visit a place I had in mind. I asked Gene if he would be willing to go with me to one of the wonders of NOLA. Gene said of course he would and reminded me that he appreciated me taking the lead in planning things for us to do.

We headed to bed and didn't discuss the looming sadness we were both feeling in knowing it would be our last time together until we could figure things out. As I laid my head on Gene's shoulder, my mind kept replaying the way he proposed to me and it thrilled me. I couldn't help but stare at the gorgeous bracelet on my wrist and still couldn't believe it; I was engaged for the first time in my life and here I was in my mid-60s. That night, I was forever young.

In the morning, we headed over to *Café Du Monde*. While enjoying our coffee, I told Gene I thoroughly enjoyed the time when he took all of us down to the tree at the end of the Wilcox property back in Naples. So, I thought he would like to experience seeing a special tree uptown in Audubon Park. It was a couple of miles away so we went over to an area by the French Market where we could hire a taxi driver to take us to *Etienne de Bore' Oak*, otherwise known as "The Tree of Life."

When we arrived at our destination, we told the taxi driver we would be about 10 minutes and asked him to wait for us. I took Gene by the hand and we walked over to the enormous live oak with Spanish moss hanging down from its massive branches. Gene was in awe of the magnificent tree. I explained to him that the tree refused to be uprooted, no matter what the obstacle, which embodies the soul of NOLA. It is a symbol of the resiliency of NOLA despite floods and hurricanes, and could possibly be hundreds of years old.

While we were there, we saw a young couple approach the tree close to where we were standing. We exchanged pleasantries and they explained they were there to plan the wedding ceremony they would be having at the "Tree of Life" in a few weeks. Gene wished them well with their upcoming nuptials and said to them, "Just like this amazing tree, obstacles come up in all our lives – just don't let things uproot your commitment to each other. Love is for the young and the old – it is for everyone. Love does not discriminate." The couple shook our hands and thanked Gene for his words of wisdom. I just stood there amazed by my man and again thanked God for bringing him into my life. After our encounter with the young couple, it really sank in – we were going to be married, in our own Gene-Pierre manner!

The taxi driver brought us back to the French Market. We walked over to Jackson Square and sat on our bench for an hour talking about our future. Neither of us wanted to wait long to start our new life together. We planned that I would return to Naples in a few months and we would have some type of ceremony to make our commitment to each other official. We knew it would have to be a scaled-down party without much publicity as it would not be possible for us to legally wed. But we were both determined to make it happen, just not sure what we could make happen.

It was getting late and Greg would be coming to pick us up to take us to the train station so we headed back to my house. There I was, taking another bittersweet walk with my Gene. Bitter because he would be leaving me, sweet because I knew we would be spending the rest of our lives together; somehow, someway.

When Greg and Michele picked us up, we were all in a somber mood. We made small talk discussing the wonderful time we all had the week that Michele and Gene were with us. All of us agreed it went by too quickly and wished it wasn't ending. When we arrived at the station, I hugged Michele goodbye and told her I looked forward to seeing her back in Naples sometime within the next few months. It was painful for me to be sending Gene off knowing our relationship was going to have to be a long distance one for quite some time. But the look of despair on Michele's face broke my heart. She did not want to be leaving Greg. I couldn't take away the pain she was feeling. However, I thought I could offer her some relief from her anguish when I took her aside and confided to her that I would be going back to Naples in about two months and I would be asking Greg to accompany me. I didn't explain to her why this would be happening, but I asked her to trust me. She thanked me profusely for acknowledging her profound sadness of having to leave the man she said she was falling in love with.

Gene took me into his strong arms and nestled his head in my neck. Then when he went to kiss me, I saw he had tears in his eyes. He seemed to be taking his leaving me with a very heavy heart. I cupped his face in my hands and said, "Please don't be sad since we will be together again in two months. With our secure love, we could get through just about anything." We agreed that each Sunday, he would call me at *Liberté*. Lil' M and Tee had recently had a telephone installed there for business purposes. Since there was an hour time difference between NOLA and Naples, I would be waiting for his call at noon. Although we would continue our letter writing, we would also be able to hear each other's voices and connect in that personal way. As the train rolled away from the platform, I waved to Gene who smiled back at me. He also touched his heart with his hand and then extended it out in my direction. I truly felt loved by my man.

The ride back to my house with Greg was just as melancholy as the ride to the station. He told me he loved Michele and he didn't know what to do about it, geographically. He confided in me that he never felt this way before and it was heart-wrenching for him to see her go back to Naples. Greg quickly composed himself and said he would like to change the subject. I felt it was time for me to tell him that Gene asked me to marry him. I explained that for obvious reasons, it wouldn't be an actual wedding but we were committed to each other and we were going to figure something out. Greg pulled over to the side of the road and gave me a tight hug. He just looked at me and said, "Pierre, I couldn't be happier for you. I believe Gene is a good man and I can tell by the way he looks at you, he truly loves you. One day I hope to have the same type of relationship you and Gene have with my precious Michele. I hope you have some whiskey at your house because I would love to come in and share a congratulatory drink with you when I drop you off."

SOMETHING OLD,
SOMETHING NEW…

Although we were forced to comply with the rules prohibiting mixed-race marriage in our country, it didn't mean we had to embrace them. We could have found someone to marry us, however, it still wouldn't be legally recognized. Therefore, we would have what we call a "union." The definition of union is the act of being joined especially in a political context. The word was perfect to describe our upcoming non-legal marriage.

After discussing it with Gene over the telephone, I sent a telegram to Charles Watkins asking him if he would officiate our union in Naples. Since he was an attorney, we felt he could bring some legality to our ceremony, although not in an official capacity. We wanted it to be as close to an actual civil wedding ceremony as possible.

To my delight, I received a telegram back that stated, "Miss Pierre, I would be honored to be the officiant at your special union."

I spent the next couple of months preparing for our union ceremony that would take place the first week of April. Gene and I decided on having a barn dance instead of a dinner at a hotel or restaurant. He asked Anna if she would be amenable to our having a dinner/dance at the grape farm where we could invite family and friends. Anna told him she would be delighted to host our union.

With the venue being figured out, the next thing needing to be done was to purchase the perfect union dress! I asked my friend Mary Grace if she would go with me to Rebecca's boutique. It was at that time I realized when a woman is preparing for her union day, she needs her girlfriends! Mary Grace enthusiastically agreed and we walked over to the boutique. Upon entering, Rebecca gave both of us a warm hug and said I looked like I was glowing. I explained to her about my upcoming union with Gene in Naples and that I needed the perfect dress to wear on my special day. She told us to take our time looking around and while we were doing that, she would open a bottle of champagne for the three of us to share. She said a celebration was called for! We were not expecting her generosity but we enthusiastically accepted! It would be the first time for me to celebrate my engagement with my girlfriends.

It didn't take more than a few minutes for me to set my eyes on a stupendous, yet simple cream dress. The color of it would bring out the flecks of green in my eyes and my darker skin tone. I could envision myself in it with my hair in an updo. Rebecca said she would bring it into the dressing room for me to try on. To my disappointment, the dress was a bit too tight through the bosom area but I loved it. I knew it was THE dress. I came out to show them how it looked. Fortunately, Rebecca said that her seamstress could add some additional fabric to the dress and it would then fit me perfectly. Both ladies said how phenomenal it looked on me. Based on their feedback and my love of the garment, I said yes to the dress!

Now that I found my dress, my mind started to think of the traditional rhyme, "Something old, something new, something borrowed, something blue and a sixpence in her shoe." I told the ladies I had a pair of cream shoes I had purchased a few years ago for a special engagement. They would be a perfect accompaniment to the dress and would be the something old. The something new, borrowed and blue would be something I still had time to find. Mary Grace insisted she wanted to buy me my something new. We spent some time admiring all the gorgeous accessories Rebecca had in her shop. I let out a little sigh when I saw a simple but elegant hair clip that was adorned with gold stones. Mary Grace came running over and asked Rebecca to box it up before I could protest!

About a week later, I went back to Rebecca's boutique

for my dress fitting with the alterations that had been made. When I tried it on, I was so relieved that it fit! I gave it back to Rebecca and asked her to box it up. I immediately took the dress back home as I didn't want to take a chance of anything happening to it. While taking it out of the box to hang in my closet, I was surprised to see an envelope with a couple of items inside it along with a note that read, "Pierre, I know you still need something blue to go along with your thought process for what every bride should have to wear on her wedding day. However, I took the liberty of giving you a purple garter rather than a blue one. After all, we are from NOLA! Also, the sixpence is for you to put in your shoe on your wedding day as a symbol of prosperity. You go girl!"

Rebecca's gesture brought a smile to my face. With her providing me the something blueish and the sixpence, the only other item I would need to incorporate into my union day attire would be something borrowed.

Gene used his spare time to clean out the barn and get it all spruced up for our big day. I felt it was the perfect time for me to thank Anna for her generously letting us have our festivities on her property. I sent her a letter letting her know how much we appreciated having a barn dance at the grape farm. I also asked her if she would be willing to be my maid of honor. Within a week I received a letter back from Anna. Her written words filled me with elation – "Pierre, I consider you to be somewhat of a mother, sister and most importantly very good friend. I would be honored to be your maid of honor." She also wrote about how things were going with her and her family. To my delight, she ended her letter with an offer to lend me a set of beautiful, golden shoe clips, which were her mother's, that I could wear on my union day. Again, Anna had the ability to know just what I needed!

Time was passing quickly leading up to my departure back to Naples. Although I was so happy to be preparing for the union between Gene and me, I couldn't help but get infuriated and frustrated by the fact that we could not legally wed. Even more upsetting was that the miscegenation laws made it a criminal offense for interracial marriages. Another thing bothering me was that I knew Johnny, Tee and Maria would not be able to travel back to Naples for our ceremony. They didn't want Maria to miss a week of school and they both had singing engagements booked. Therefore, Gene and I decided we would have a special event in NOLA in the early summer so we could celebrate with them. Knowing that lessened my sadness. The one person who I felt I could discuss just about anything with, was Greg. I needed to share with him what I was going through. We met at Jackson Square and he just let me talk. We both knew he couldn't do anything to change the situation regarding my inability to legally wed, however, he did point out that the only way I could make it better for myself was to take control of the way I would deal with the unfairness of our situation. What Greg said made sense and just talking about my frustrations with him put me in a better place. He was my rock and I needed my rock with me on my union day. It was the perfect time for me to ask a favor of him. I said, "Would you be willing to go to Naples with me for a week to help Gene and me get ready for our big day? Your being there with me would put me at ease and give me the support I need. You have that effect on me, Greg. Since I have met you, you have become a support system."

Greg told me he would need a couple of days to see if he could get a week off from his job at the newspaper before he could give me an answer. I told him to take his time and get back to me when he could but I wanted to pay for his train ticket if he could go. It was the least I could do.

A week later Greg came over to my house with a bag. I knew exactly what was in it and appreciated him bringing the whiskey! After I poured each of us a drink, he told me he was sorry but he couldn't get a week off from work to go with me to Naples. I admitted to him I was disappointed but I understood his predicament. He said although he couldn't go, he could give me a ride to the train station on the day I would be leaving. I gladly accepted his offer and we talked a great deal about his relationship with Michele. Greg said, "Pierre, she is the woman I never thought I would meet. One day I hoped to find someone I would love and possibly have a family with. That just never happened for me in NOLA. Perhaps I spent too much time focusing on my career with the *New Orleans Observer.* I do love my job as a reporter. However, I think I might love her more. I haven't told her all of this yet and I am only speculating that she feels the same way. I know you and Gene are able to have a long-distance romance. But it just won't work for me, especially since I am hoping she too wants a family. We are going to have to have a serious talk the next time we are together. She is planning to come here in the early summer and I am already counting the days."

OUR UNION DAY

I was so excited when the day finally arrived for me to leave to go to Naples to be with Gene and start our new lives together! Johnny, Tee and Maria came to see me in the morning to wish me well on my trip and to congratulate me on my upcoming union with Gene. We discussed that while I was away for a few weeks, it would be the perfect time for them to move their belongings over to their new house; our house. This way, when I returned, we would all be together under one roof.

Greg came to my house promptly at the time we had agreed upon. Once we arrived at the train station, he parked in the lot, got out of his auto and brought out my suitcase and put it on the platform. He went back and took out another suitcase that he placed next to mine. I looked at Greg inquisitively and he said, "I hope you don't mind, but I will be accompanying you back to Naples. Your son Johnny asked me to fill in for him, giving you away at your union. I told him I would be honored." For a few moments I was speechless. But then I asked him how he was able to get the time off from his job. Greg said, "Some things are more important than work. So, I went to the editor-in-chief of the newspaper and told him since I couldn't have a week off to travel back to Naples, I would be resigning!" Much to my surprise, he said, "Greg, take the week off with my blessing. You have done an outstanding job with the "Perseverance of Pierre" articles. We don't want to lose your superlative journalistic contributions to the newspaper. Your future here is secure and you will be receiving a pay raise. I will see you when you return from your trip." Greg chuckled and told me he never thought being prepared to resign would be the best career move he ever made!

The almost three-day train ride was enjoyable. I was able to relax, admire the picturesque scenery of the landscapes rolling by my window and just live in the moment. Greg and I spent some of the time together. However, we also spent time on our own. Many stops and hours later we rolled into the station. Both of us were glad to see our loves waiting on the platform. As soon as the door opened, I ran into Gene's arms and we kissed like two teenagers in love for the first time.

Greg and Michele left us at the station. She was taking Greg to meet her parents. I thought to myself that Greg didn't need to worry about Michele's commitment to a future with him; she was all in. Greg's parting words to

Gene and me were, "We are so looking forward to your union in a couple of days. The two of you have made me believe that love can happen and thrive, no matter what. The key is perseverance!"

The next two days were joyous while we were putting the final touches on all the aspects of our union and barn dance. I appreciated that Gene had taken care of getting our rings and making sure the menu and set up for the event were all worked out with the staff from the Naples Hotel. He was a man who could take charge! That was one of the many things I loved about him.

On the afternoon of our special day, the ceremony was to take place in the living room of the main house. Anna had the room filled with bouquets of pink roses and candles were lit throughout the room. There was an understated elegance with those simple touches. I was asked to wait in my room until I heard my song, "Lace Around the Moon" playing. That was my cue to come out. Greg was waiting for me at my bedroom door. We locked arms as he escorted me a few steps over to Gene. The only other guests present were Anna, my maid of honor; Peter, Gene's best man and Michele.

Charles Watkins did a splendid job officiating our union. Any outsider witnessing the event would not have any reason to doubt its authenticity. He used the standard script that was recited at most weddings and Gene and I added in our own words. We took each other's hands and Gene said, "Pierre, you have become my best friend, lover and now wife. I will honor our union and will cherish you until my dying day. Forever thine, forever mine, forever us. I securely love you."

In turn, I said to Gene, "Until I met you, I never stopped to smell the grapes. You have taught me what it is to be loved and how to give love. As written by the poet Omar Khayyám, "Be happy for this moment. This moment is your life." Please know I am so happy for this moment with you and look forward to spending our lives together. I securely love you."

We exchanged gold bands each with a green and purple stone on them. For us, they represented the colors of NOLA and the purple also expressed our appreciation of the grapes.

Charles said, "I now pronounce you man and wife. Gene, you may kiss your bride!" After we shared our first kiss as a "unioned" couple, we embraced those who were there with us. Gene and I couldn't stop smiling. We shared a private look between us; both knowing that we were breaking man-made rules on many levels and we reveled in it. Peter opened up a bottle of champagne and poured us each a glass. He offered us a toast, "Congratulations

Pierre and Gene. We are all so happy you have found each other. I feel there is abundant love in this room – *Laissez les bons temps rouler!*"

When the champagne was finished, we headed over to the barn. The staff from the Naples Hotel did a phenomenal job of setting the main barn area up to look like a fancy supper club. It was absolutely breathtaking. For our union gift, Anna hired the same band that performed at the Jazz Jam. The music started as soon as we walked in and continued for the next three hours. It was a party with over 100 guests!

The food the staff had prepared and served was amazing. There were different food areas set up around the perimeter of the barn. That way the guests could graze on different food items at their leisure which included a meat station of roast beef, chicken and deer. There was also a special table with red beans and rice and jambalaya. It was a "union" of foods! There was plenty of wine and grape juice for everyone! For dessert, instead of a wedding cake, we had apple and grape pies!

An hour into the party, Gene and I asked everyone to raise their glasses in a toast. I said, "I would like to share a quote from poet Khyyám's Rubáiyát that I also used with friends earlier in the day, "Drink wine. This is life eternal. This is all that youth will give you. It is the season for wine, roses and drunken friends. Be happy for this moment." Gene and I are forever grateful to all of you for being with us and hope that you are as happy as we are for this moment."

The day was amazing and the thing that will stay in my mind forever was when Gene asked me to come outside. Since it was cold out I didn't particularly relish having to leave the warmth of the barn. But I put my Ellis jacket on and he led me out the side door. While standing out in the driveway, I couldn't believe what I was seeing. There was white fluffy snow coming down from the skies. Gene and I stood there looking up with our mouths open as the white glistening flakes tickled my tongue. I took that as a sign that it was meant to be – Gene and me – forever, in secure love.

After we came in from our snowflake-tasting adventure, our guests started to come to say goodbye. First was Charles Watkins. He hugged both Gene and me and thanked us for a wonderful afternoon. His skin was clammy and he didn't look very good. I asked him if he was feeling okay and he said his diabetes was getting the best of him. I told Charles I was sorry he wasn't feeling well and asked him if he was up for driving home. He assured us he would be fine as soon as he got home, took his medicine and got some rest.

Shortly after Charles' departure, our other guests

also left including Anna and Peter. Since they were at the grape farm early in the morning, they were anxious to get home and see their babies. We thanked them profusely for all they did for us. I told Anna she was the best maid of honor a woman could have asked for. Gene shook Peter's hand and told him he too did a fantastic job of being his best man!

At the very end, it was just Greg, Michele and us. We shared a final drink before saying goodbye. I hugged Greg and thanked him for everything! He said he would see me back in NOLA. Gene and I hugged Michele and I told her I looked forward to seeing her in NOLA in the summer, when she comes for a visit to see Greg. I whispered in her ear, "If your heart is open, so is Greg's. I see the two of you together. Perhaps that is presumptuous of me to say. But I have learned – to say what needs to be said when you have the opportunity. Otherwise, it may be too late and then there are regrets."

The staff from the Naples Hotel were almost finished cleaning up the barn and were ready to leave. We thanked them for the stupendous job they did and gave them a generous gratuity. It was then I felt I could let my hair down and relax. Gene and I sat down to decompress and share a glass of wine. We were exhilarated yet exhausted from the day we were blessed to have. It was getting late so we left the barn and walked over to the main house, hand in hand. We were both looking forward to our first night as man and wife.

All the while Gene and I were in our courtship, we would sleep in the bed I would use when I stayed at the grape farm. However, on our union night, I accompanied him to his bed. Gene held me tight and whispered in my ear, "Good night my wife, I securely love you." Everything just felt so right!

IRISH BLESSINGS

The following day, Gene and I loaded up his auto and we headed to our honeymoon destination in Buffalo, NY. Gene asked me the previous month if he could plan our honeymoon getaway. I told him that anything he came up with would be fine with me, as long as it didn't involve me cooking or cleaning.

It was about a two-hour drive to the Shamrock Inn, located in Buffalo. The proprietor, Mary Ann Malloy welcomed us with open arms. The inn was decorated with an Irish motif and had a very inviting atmosphere. She had a lovely wine and cheese spread set up for us in her living room. While we were enjoying the delectable nibbles, wine and grape juice, she shared an Irish Toast – "May those who love us love us. And those that don't love us, May God turn their hearts. And if he doesn't turn their hearts, may he turn their ankles, so we'll know them by their limping." I knew at that moment I could be friends with this woman; she had spunk!

Gene proudly professed that he had some Irish blood

in him and that he liked her Irish toast. We asked her if she would share some of the background on her Shamrock Inn and a bit about her life. Mary Ann explained that after she retired from her governmental job, she wanted to do something to occupy her time and celebrate her Irish heritage. So, she purchased the four-bedroom house and had it converted into the Inn. She loved the location since it was across the street from one of the landmark parks in the Buffalo area. The Park, located in the northwest section of Buffalo within Erie County, New York, was designed and developed by Federick Law Olmstead and Calvert Vaux between 1868 and 1876. The 350-acre park was created as a "country park" to provide beautiful and restorative scenery to counteract the stress of urban life. The Park's landscape was designed by Olmstead, who is known as the grandfather of American landscape architecture and who also designed New York City's Central Park.

She gave us a tour of her property and showed us to our room. Mary Ann explained that breakfast, lunch and dinner were included in the cost of our stay. She loved to cook and entertain people in her home so she went over her menu with us for the next three days. Everything she suggested sounded divine. I was just so glad I would not have to do any domestic chores.

Gene and I explored the property and neighborhood.

But we spent most of our time talking; really talking. We hadn't had a lot of face-to-face time with each other since we became involved, less than a year ago and I felt that with no other distractions around us, we truly got to know each other over those three days.

On the last day of our stay, we went over to the Park. We spent a few hours walking around, then had a picnic lunch at Mirror Lake that Mary Ann prepared. The tranquility I felt there reminded me of Jackson Square back in NOLA. Olmstead had succeeded in making the Park a place for relaxation, with its serene beauty all around. Rather than discuss our future over lunch, we just lived in the moment that day. I was proud of myself when I realized, that is the way life should be lived. It just took me being with Gene to make that happen!

The following morning, we went downstairs to the kitchen for our last meal at the Shamrock Inn. Mary Ann made us a wonderful breakfast of corned beef hash, fried eggs and Irish soda bread. After serving us some Irish coffee, she gave us another Irish blessing – "May the sun shine warm upon your face, the rains fall soft upon your fields. And until we meet again, may God hold you in the palm of his hand." I told Mary Ann I enjoyed all of her Irish sayings and blessings and that the one on the back of our bedroom door was my favorite: "May you be in heaven an hour before the devil knows you dead." I asked her what she thought the saying meant. She said, "My takeaway is that we all wish to live a quiet life so when we die, we can sneak off to heaven even though we may have secrets in our lives. You don't want the devil to come looking for you!" She then gave us a quick wink and a hug.

After we finished eating, Gene brought our bags from our room down to his auto.

The three of us walked outside and we thanked Mary Ann for everything she did to make our honeymoon getaway so incredible. We also promised Mary Ann that each year on our anniversary, we would come back to spend some time there. We both felt a connection to her and the Shamrock Inn. It will forever hold a special place in our hearts since it was the first place we went to after we entered into our union. Mary Ann accepted us into her home without prejudice. She didn't see the color of skin. She just saw the color of green which was apparent throughout her home. Every room was decorated in green! Mary Ann explained that the color green represents rebirth, health, hope and many positive things related to overall well-being. I definitely felt the positivity at the Shamrock Inn.

On our ride home to Naples, we didn't talk a great deal. Both of us seemed to be lost in thought. So much happened in less than a year and it was an opportunity for us to relive the moments of our whirlwind courtship and union in our minds. It was so comforting to be sitting next to the man I love and just be in his presence without exchanging words. It was the most amazing connection I ever had with another person without conversing. This man was my Irish blessing!

HIDDEN SECRETS

Before we knew it, we were pulling into the driveway of the grape farm and were surprised to see Anna and Peter's autos. Gene and I started to take out our bags and carry them into the house. When we entered the kitchen, Anna and Peter were sitting at the table and they looked very upset. I asked them what was wrong. Anna said, "We didn't want to bother you while you were on your honeymoon, so we waited until your return to tell you both some sad news. Charles Watkins is in the hospital and he is not doing well. The day after the union party, his secretary and her husband found him in his home, unresponsive. They were able to get him to the hospital, where the staff was able to revive him. However, he is drifting in and out of consciousness. Apparently, he has not been taking insulin for his diabetes on a regular schedule and the excessive drinking is making it worse. Anna said, "Pierre, would you please come with me to the hospital? I would appreciate it and I think he would find some peace in seeing you."

Anna and I left Gene and Peter behind at the farm and she drove us to the hospital. Upon entering his room, I was saddened to see how frail he looked lying there in his hospital bed. Anna went over to him and took his hand. He opened his eyes briefly and smiled at her. My heart was breaking for him knowing he may die with never having had the opportunity to tell Anna that he was her father. I made a life-changing decision at that moment, which I may not have had the right to do. However, I was willing to take the fallout since I considered it necessary for Anna to know that Charles was most likely her father. My decision was based on the fact that Charles' diabetes could possibly be hereditary and Anna needed to know that for herself and her children.

I asked Anna to leave the room for one minute so I could talk privately with Charles. She seemed confused by my request but did as I asked. When we were alone, I pleaded with Charles to tell Anna that he was her father. Tears welled out of his eyes and he just looked at me. I made out his words through his hoarse voice. He said he physically and emotionally didn't have it in him to do so. However, he asked me if I would please tell her for him. I was stunned at his request and not sure I was comfortable doing so. However, if I wouldn't do that for him, and do it for Anna, it might not have ever been done. With a surge of strength and fortitude out of the love I had for Anna, I told Charles I would do as he requested. My thought was I would be the conduit not of his deathbed confession but rather his deathbed concession.

I held Charles' hand for a minute before I left the room, with the feeling it was the last time I would ever see him. As I walked over to Anna, she looked up at me with tears in her eyes. It hurt me to see her in the quandary she appeared to be in. Since there was no one around us, I felt I could tell her what I had to say without anyone else overhearing our conversation. I sat down next to her and said, "Anna, Charles has asked me to tell you something. Since he isn't physically able to tell you himself, I told him I would be his voice. It doesn't make sense for me to sugarcoat my words since I feel it is imperative to give you this information straight and to the point, even if it is upsetting. And since we don't know Charles' medical prognosis, time is of the essence.

Many years ago, when your parents were not able to conceive a child, they asked Charles to try and impregnate your mother. They wanted a child so badly, that they were willing to do whatever they could to make it happen, even if it was immoral and wrong on many levels. They were desperate and felt they had no other options. The choice the three of them made to make your and Phillip's birth happen was unconventional, to say the least. But you must believe that how you and Phillip were conceived was out of love, just not out of love between a man and a woman; a third man was involved. Your parents truly loved each other, they just couldn't make a family on their own. I hope you understand that Charles truly loves you. He just never felt he could tell you he was your father because he promised your parents he would never tell anyone. Charles is a man of his word and I have come to respect him for the choices he made and the promises he kept. However, with him being so sickly with diabetes, he believes you need to know his paternal status relating to you."

Anna was silent for a moment as she let it all sink in. I was prepared to offer her whatever emotional support she would need. Much to my surprise, she blurted out, "My God Pierre, I am relieved to hear he may be my father. I can't tell you why, but as I shared with you previously, I always felt that my father was not my father. As much as I am saddened to find out that may be the truth, I finally have a sense of closure. All my life I thought I was crazy to think there was just not the father-daughter connection I should have had with my father. At one point, when I was an adult, I wanted to confront my mother about my suspicions. But since my mother and father were killed in a car crash many years ago, I never had the opportunity."

Anna took a deep breath and thanked me for telling her all of the information. She said she realized it was a lot that Charles put on me and she really appreciated what I had done. She got up from her chair and left me to go into Charles' room. She needed private time with him; father and daughter time. While I was sitting in the waiting room, I was surprised but relieved beyond words to see Peter and Gene approaching me. Gene said he had a feeling I might need him. He opened his arms as I went to him and put my head on his shoulder. His embrace was the comfort I was so in need of. Although I was glad I was there for Anna and Charles in their time of need, I was drained from the entire experience. But I had peace in knowing I did a good thing in bringing a father and daughter together.

Having my own emotional needs taken care of, I hugged Peter and assured him Anna was fine. I explained that she was with Charles having a conversation that may be overwhelming to her. However, I told him I felt she could handle whatever was being discussed. She may just need some extra compassion and support to deal with what she is going through.

At that point, I felt I could leave with Gene. It didn't make any sense for me to stay since Peter was there to take care of Anna. We asked him if he needed anything before we left. He said he was fine and thanked us for being there for him and Anna. As we were walking away, I said, "You and Anna are my northern family. Please get in touch with us when you are ready, we will be there for both of you."

When we got into Gene's auto, he said, "If and when you want to discuss any of what happened, I am there for you. But I respect your privacy and will not bring it up again unless you do. Let's get home so I can make you supper and get you a glass of wine so we can both unwind. That night as we fell asleep, I felt I had a better understanding of what secure love meant. I had never been more secure or in love in my life.

Early in the morning, we heard voices in the living room. We both quickly dressed and went to see who was there. It was Anna and Peter and the twins, in their playpen. Anna asked if she could talk to me in private. We went out on the front porch while Gene and Peter headed into the kitchen. Gene said he would put coffee on for anyone who wanted some. Anna again thanked me for uniting her and Charles. She said, "I told Peter that I learned Charles was most likely my father, not Henry Wilcox, and that I believed it to be true. Peter was so wonderful and comforting to me without pushing me for more information about this convoluted situation. We talked things through and decided we would not be sharing this information with anyone other than you and Gene. We want it to be a secret only between the four of us. That is why we are here. Would you please explain everything to Gene for me, as I don't have the stamina to even try. Peter and I need to head to the hospital. I promised Charles I would bring the twins to him as soon as possible since he was not doing well, and fear it may be the last time..."

After Anna, Peter and the twins left, I poured us a cup of coffee. Although I knew Gene needed to go work in the fields, I asked him to please sit down for a minute as there was something he needed to hear from me. Starting from when I first met Charles months ago until yesterday, I explained how he became Anna and Phillip's biological father. Gene looked at me when I finished speaking and took my hand. He said, "Life has many twists and turns. No one has the right to judge others for the decisions they make. What you just shared with me will be kept between us. It is not any of my business, but I am glad you shared it with me as I am sure it was something that has weighed heavily on your mind."

After Gene left to go work the fields, I went to lie down for a bit to just decompress. Since I was so emotionally spent, I quickly fell asleep. When I woke up a few hours later, there was the smell of something heavenly being cooked. I sat down and Gene said, "Anna was here but she didn't want to wake you. She wanted us to know Charles passed away peacefully a short time after she was able to take the twins to see him."

I sat there for a few minutes in silence collecting my thoughts. Gene asked me if I would like a cup of tea. My response was, "If you will join me, a whiskey would be more appropriate at this time." He poured us both a glass. I said, "From everything that came out over the past two days, I learned you can live your life with secrets but you can't die peacefully with them. You have to come to terms with them and profess them before you can pass. If only we could all do that before we come to death's door, then the door to our salvation or passing over wouldn't be so heavy to slip through and then close. I believe I was in the right place at the right time to help him cross over. Rest in peace, Charles."

LIFE GOES ON

Gene and I were saddened by Charles' passing, but life still goes on. The next couple of days at the farm were simple and easy. Gene and I took walks through the vineyard. But now with our union and honeymoon over, we needed to decide how we would move forward. We discussed buying a small house in Naples near the farm so he could continue to manage the daily operations. However, after really thinking it through, that didn't seem to make financial sense. Since Anna always made him feel as though the main house was his to use for as long as he wanted to, we decided he would just continue to live there until we had a finalized plan for our future.

After discussing it further, we came to the decision that despite the geographical restrictions, we would make efforts to be together physically whenever possible. However, we will always remain connected in our hearts. We agreed to continue to visit each other in our respective cities, ensuring that we would be together, though separately, a significant amount of the time. Gene said, "Pierre, I believe if we work at it, it will work."

With the "for the time being" talk out of the way, I felt better. However, I was missing my family and NOLA. Gene sensed my longing for them and he made it easy for me when he said that he would like to take me to the train station and purchase my return ticket to NOLA. He said we could do it mid-week before we went to Charles Watkins' memorial service. We decided I would leave over the upcoming weekend.

One afternoon when Gene was busy in the vineyard, I walked over to the berry-picker house. I was thinking a lot about Charles and felt the need to read the message he had written on the wall all those years ago when he impregnated Lillian. "Forgive me, Father, for I have sinned." That one sentence was so life-changing for Anna and me. I also read over the words I put on the wall back when I first came to Naples to attend Phillip's trial. It was my message to Phillip, telling him how I had given up my son, but that he had become the son I never had the pleasure of knowing. How blessed I was that within a year of that message, Johnny came into my life. It made me think that by writing things on the wall of the berry-picker house, there was some type of energy or special force that somehow could absolve Charles and myself of our past indiscretions or choices.

Words are so powerful, especially written words, and they can set things in motion. They are also difficult to take back. With that process, I decided I would leave a little message for Gene. I hoped one day he would find it and read it. There was a pencil on the little table. I picked it up and wrote my message in the opposite corner of Charles' message. It simply read, "Gene, I securely love you. Pierre." My feelings for the man were all wrapped up in those few, powerful words.

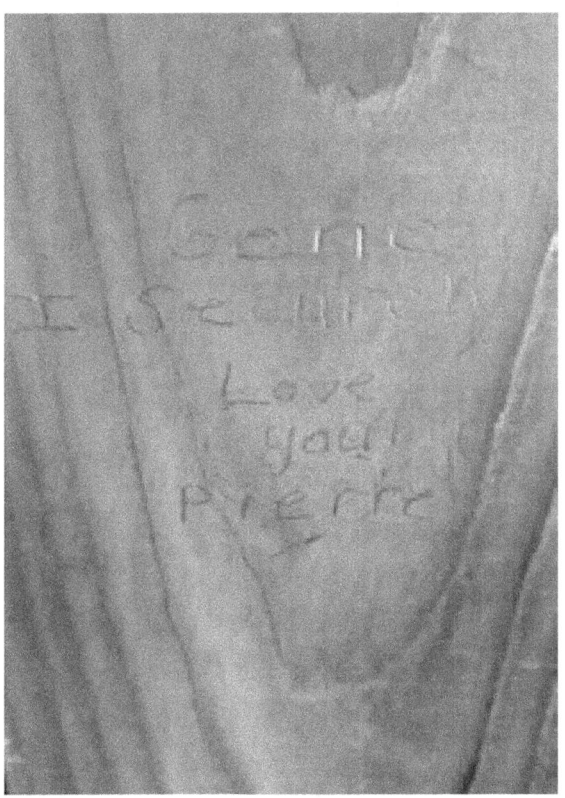

Our time together over the next couple days went by quickly. Before we knew it, it was time to meet Anna and Peter at a local church for the memorial service. Charles had been an elder in the congregation for many years and they wanted to hold his service. There was even a breakfast afterward in their social area. It made me happy to see so many people attend the service to pay their respects. Dan and Lori Manno and Gene's sister Terry and her husband Rick sat in our row. The Arno family was there along with Michele and her step-brother, Judge Higby who sat in the row behind us. The room was jam-packed and the preacher did a lovely job of celebrating the man's life. When it ended, most of the participants headed over to the breakfast. Later in the day, there would be a private burial where Charles would be laid to rest next to his departed wife, Mary. Anna and I talked for a few minutes before she had to excuse herself to deal with an issue with the catering. She confided to me that she and Peter took care of the service and breakfast. She felt it was the least she could do for her father. Since she had only learned about the entire situation within the last week, she still hadn't had time to process everything. Anna asked me if just the two of us could talk before I headed back to NOLA. I reached for her and she put her head on my shoulder but only for a brief moment. I said, "When you are ready, we will talk and just know I am here for you with whatever you may need. I have your back. Just think of when we had our girl's night at the Naples Hotel. We will see each other through any challenges that come our way."

I was able to see Anna, Peter and their babies before I left. Those precious twins filled me with such joy. It was too hard to say the word goodbye to all of them so I told them I would just see them when I returned in the fall. Gene and I still had a couple of days together before he would be taking me to the train station. We made the most of our remaining time, making it meaningful and special.

The day of my departure was difficult for both of us, but we knew it was inevitable. Although we were secure in our love for each other, our relationship was not one for the faint of heart; it was heart-wrenching.

We pulled into the train station and parked. Gene helped me with my suitcases. We embraced and made sure our hearts touched. Simple "I love you" words were exchanged and I got onto the train. Neither of us wanted to have a long, drawn-out goodbye session. Sometimes the sharpest knife cuts the quickest. Why prolong the misery?

I slept most of the time on the train ride back to NOLA. When I arrived, Greg and Johnny were there to greet me. The feeling of home enfolded me and took my breath away. For a brief moment, I questioned whether I would ever be able to leave NOLA. It didn't make sense to dwell on that thought so I moved on from it. Greg drove Johnny and me home. It was my first night with Johnny, Tee, and Maria under one roof.

MOVING FORWARD

The next couple of weeks were jam-packed with activity. One of the remaining items I didn't get to take care of before my union was going to Maria's school. But with the school year soon coming to a close, I thought it would be the right time to go and make my proposal. I didn't have an appointment when I showed up and asked if I could speak to the principal. Fortunately, the secretary recognized me and said, "Miss Pierre, I am honored to meet you. Please have a seat and I will see if our principal is available." It was only a few minutes before a very robust-looking gentleman came over to me and introduced himself as Mr. Bourdeaux. He shook my hand and asked if I would like to follow him into his office. Mr. Bourdeaux said he was pleased to meet me and that he has enjoyed my music over the years. I thanked him for his acknowledgment and told him I didn't want to take up too much of his time. However, there was something I needed to speak with him about.

In thinking over the best way to approach him about

this event, I decided to follow the thought process of "You get more bees with honey than vinegar." I could have told him about the bullying Maria experienced by some of her schoolmates calling her derogatory names due to her fair skin and freckles. Instead, I said, "I believe you know that Maria, one of your 8th grade students, is my grandchild. We have discussed how much her education means to her. Therefore, I would like to know if you would be agreeable to me having a small singing event at your institution before the summer break. It would be a simple affair with me singing a few of my popular songs and inviting the students to join in. I believe it will bring a favorable light to your school and help to bond your students in song." Mr. Bourdeaux just smiled and said he thought that would be a wonderful way to bring the students and faculty together. He even suggested we have the event as soon as possible. I thought about it for a minute and told him I could have it all set up and ready to go in two weeks. We again shook hands and I also asked if he would welcome me bringing in refreshments for the event. He actually laughed and said, "You are not only a talented singer Miss Pierre, you are also a wise woman. You realize the way to children's hearts is through their stomachs! Yes, thank you so much for offering to have refreshments on the special day of our school coming together in food and song."

When I left Maria's school, I went over to see Flordie

at her bakery. We discussed me having a sing-along at Maria's school and I asked her if I could hire her to make sweet treats and light refreshments for the event. Flordie gladly accepted my business proposal. There was one special request I asked of her in deciding what desserts she would make. As a subtle way of silently proving my point that you get more bees with honey, I asked her if she would prepare the delectables using honey rather than sugar. She said she would do that and didn't even ask me why.

Two weeks later, the staff and students of Maria's school assembled in their cafeteria, where I performed in the front of the room. The children all seemed to enjoy singing along with the songs. However, that was not the main event. I never told Principal Bourdeaux what I had planned to do. After I sang my last song, I asked Maria to come up and join me. We held hands and performed "Christmas Dishes" together a cappella. I sang the standard verses and Maria sang the chorus. After finishing, we hugged each other and took a bow. The entire room erupted in applause. Several of the students ran up to Maria and congratulated her on her performance and no one said, "Hi Yellow Maria." They all wanted to be her friend and she was finally accepted as a black girl with reddish tints in her hair and freckles. From that day forward, Maria was seen in a different light.

The entire experience was very satisfying. I particularly enjoyed watching Mr. Bourdeaux take several trips to the table and fill his plate. With every bite he took, I relished in knowing you get more bees with honey. That day, I was the queen bee! Sometimes small victories feel the best when no one else even knew there was a war.

Another thing weighing on my mind was the crypt TCA purchased for me at the Metairie Cemetery. Having a crypt next to TCA's family crypt and where he was buried, was overwhelming and unsettling. Therefore, I decided it was time to put that matter to rest and move forward. My mind replayed my life and many of the significant things that happened to me since I first was sent to New Orleans to give birth to Johnny at the Ursuline Convent. Those thoughts included Sister Veronica, the head nun at the convent and her sister, Miss Margaret who owned the Courtesan Cottage. If it had not been for Sister Veronica, I would have been forced to go back to Mississippi and the rapes by my stepfather would have continued. If it had not been for Miss Margaret taking me under her wing and offering me a place to live, I don't know what would have happened to me. It became clear to me that I should donate my crypt to the nuns at the Ursuline Convent.

The following day, I went to the Metairie Cemetery office. The groundskeeper Richard was there and when he saw me, he gave me a warm embrace and complimented me on how well I looked. He said he read all of the articles that were in the *New Orleans Observer* about my life and was so happy for me with my singing success, especially with "Lace Around the Moon." Richard was an absolute gentleman. He offered me a seat and asked me if I wanted some water. I took him up on both of his offers. Richard proudly disclosed that he had recently been promoted to the manager of the cemetery and he would be glad to assist me in any way possible. I explained to him that I did not want to keep the crypt deeded to me by TCA. Instead, I would be contacting my attorney to have him work with the Metairie Cemetery management to have it officially deeded to the Catholic Church for the nuns at the Ursuline Convent to use as they wished. Since Richard was well aware of the entire situation, I felt I could talk openly with him. Richard just nodded his head and did not ask any further questions. I asked him if he would be able to show me some of the other available plots for sale in the cemetery, to put an above-ground crypt on for my family. He went over to his desk and pulled out what looked to be a map of the property. After a few minutes of him looking over the document, he asked if I was up for a walk over to a section of the cemetery he thought I might be interested in.

It was only a five-minute walk over to a serene, rather secluded area. He explained that it was a newer section that was being prepared for future sales. I asked him if I could have a few minutes to myself to ponder my possible purchase. He said he would be back for me in ten minutes. As I sat there in the beautiful surroundings, it didn't take me any time at all to make my decision. I believe Richard knew exactly what I was looking for when he brought me to that particular section of the cemetery. There was a sapling tree I could tell hadn't reached the height it would one day. Seeing that tree made my decision easy. Since I was a realistic woman, I knew I would not be on this earth by the time the tree reached its maturity. But knowing my family would find solace in seeing the tree shading the area where our crypt would be when they would go there for visits, gave me a sense of peace. They would be able to look up and see the tree's lace around the moon.

Richard came back for me and we walked back to the office. I told him I would like to purchase my family crypt in the location he just showed me. Since I had the money to purchase it outright, I asked him to please prepare a bill of sale and I would get him a check within the next week. He said that would be fine and he would have the management of the cemetery contact me to go over finalizing my donation to the Ursuline nuns. I could tell Richard wanted to ask me questions about what I was doing but he was too polite to. He instead embraced me again when I left his office. On my way back home,

I thought it was rather fitting that TCA was buried next to a crypt that would belong to the nuns at the Ursuline Convent; good and evil spending eternity, side by side.

That night when I went to sleep, I said a prayer thanking the dear Lord for giving me the strength I needed to accomplish all of the items on my to-do list. With all of those things behind me, I was ready to move forward.

PERSEVERANCE HALL

With continued royalties from "Lace Around the Moon," my finances were strong and there was money left over – a lot of money! I realized it would be fiscally prudent for me to work with a financial planner, to make sure I invested my money properly. My family's financial future needed to be secure. Having enough capital for Gene and my future living arrangements was also important, whatever that may be.

For years I had toyed with the idea of opening up my own jazz club. Now with my financial affairs more than secure, it could become a reality. I had a friend, Mark Lensky, who was a police officer and sold real estate in the Quarter part-time. I set up a meeting with him to discuss purchasing a piece of property I could turn into a club. Luck was on my side when he told me there was a small jazz club for sale on Burgundy Street, however, it was in foreclosure due to tax liens. We wasted no time and went to look it over. Mark explained that the building included the bar with an area that could accommodate up to 100 patrons and a decent size kitchen. It also had two rooms in the back that could be rented out. I was particularly drawn to the bar area where my mind's eye could envision different acts performing and guests seated at intimate tables with low candle lighting. I could feel the ambiance; I felt the entire place. It just needed some tender loving care and quite a bit of money! After our preliminary walk though, I wouldn't say I was disappointed but rather inspired. I saw the property as possibly becoming my labor of love, let me reiterate, "my" in the most proprietary terms. For years I worked for others in their establishments and had to follow their rules as I was only the hired talent. If the place were to become mine and then eventually Johnny and Tee's, it would be the first time in my life that I would be in control. Of course, I would ask Johnny and Tee if they would be willing to help manage it with me. But I embraced the idea of my being the "madam of the house." Just not the type of house I had worked in for many years of my life. So, with all those thoughts running through my mind, I looked past the walls that needed repairs, the floor that was buckling, the kitchen that was missing parts of the ceiling and the boarded-up windows and I saw what I would one day call, Perseverance Hall.

After looking over everything I needed to see, we walked back to his office. He was great at his job and we sat down and went over how much the property would cost, what I would have to pay in back taxes and of course his commission. He hesitantly passed me a piece of paper with the bottom line written down. I saw him gasp when I said, "Draw up the paperwork and show me where to sign!"

Mark said it would take about two weeks for him to get the deed to the property and other paperwork all compiled. He further explained it would all depend on whether I could get an approved bank loan in my name to purchase the property. I just smiled at Mark and said, "Do you know of a place around here where we can go and get a whiskey to celebrate my purchasing this unpolished gem?" He said that there was a "blind pig" a block over where he knew the owner and we could get a drink at 10:00 am. I asked him what exactly was a "blind pig". He explained that was what some people called a speakeasy during prohibition. I stood up, gathered my belongings, and said, "Let's go to the blind pig to celebrate!" Mark said he didn't want to be rude but he thought I might be a bit presumptuous to be so confident that I would be approved for the bank loan. I said, "Mark you have little faith. We are going to celebrate that I just purchased a jazz club and you will be receiving a nice commission. As long as you do your part to get all the paperwork in order, it will be a done deal. I don't require a bank loan, let's just say – all the necessary money is in the bank, actually in my bank account!"

Over our drinks at the blind pig, Mark said, "Miss Pierre, I think you are making a sound business decision and I wouldn't steer you in the wrong direction. With my many years of experience in the real estate business, I know quite a few reputable contractors and legitimate city officials whom I can recommend to get the place up to code and pass inspection. It will be a bit of a process but with my contacts, I believe you could get it up and running in three months." I thought about what he said and told him that I would like it all accomplished in two months. Although I understood that would be a large undertaking, since I had the money to pay the contractors to hire additional workers, I asked him if he thought two months could then be possible. I said, "My desire is to have it done by then so I could have the grand opening when my partner will be coming to visit me in about two months." Before he could respond, I told him there would be a substantial gratuity for him to make it happen as soon as possible, as long as that was within two months. Mark's parting words to me were, "I believe it can be done in two months. I will contact you in a week when all the paperwork will be ready for your signature. I will need your check for the property at that time along with the money for the back taxes. Your check will have to clear before we move forward. After that, I can put you in contact with some contractors I know who can start to work on bringing the property up to code and doing the work you want done. You can wait to pay my commission until all is said and done. I trust you and look forward to this business venture with you Miss Pierre!"

I went home that afternoon and sat in my back courtyard. Maria was still at school and Johnny and Tee were rehearsing at a club for a show they would be doing that evening. I poured a glass of wine from a bottle that Gene packed for me when I left Naples and sat there thinking about how my life had changed but was still evolving. My decision to purchase the club on Burgundy Street was beginning to excite me and fill me with a passion I hadn't felt since I first opened up *Liberté* with Lil' M, many years ago.

I stayed up late waiting for Johnny and Tee to return. When they arrived, I asked them if they had some time that week to go and look at a little place on Burgundy Street that I thought would be of interest to them. They both looked at me inquisitively and asked if we were moving. I didn't see the sense of dragging out the surprise so I exuberantly said, "Today I met with my realtor and made an offer on a building that was previously a jazz club but was in foreclosure. It needs a lot of work but I see it as a sound business investment for us. I would love for the two of you to take a look at it before I finalize the financial aspects of the purchase. If you see it in the same light as I did, Perseverance Hall will be ours!"

Two days later, Mark met the three of us outside of the property. After our walk-through, Johnny and Tee embraced each other and jumped up and down! I could tell by their reaction they too saw the potential in the place and were as excited as I was to make it our own. After seeing their exuberance, I changed my mind and said to Mark, "I will work with my attorney and the bank to have the deed to the property put into the three of our names. It will be a family operation right from the very beginning!"

After Johnny, Tee and I returned home, we sat down and had our first business talk. I explained that I would like them to be the managers of Perseverance Hall. It would be their responsibility to book the acts that would perform. However, I explained if there was a singer or an act that I would like to give an opportunity to, they would have to accept my request. The three of us would work out the details of the décor and ambiance we would like to present to our customers. But I told them I would like to have intimate tables set with low candle lighting. I wanted our customers to have a feel of what a true jazz club was. Our place needed to have the allure of a swanky club but be affordable to all who come through our doors. There would be no airs about Perseverance Hall; it would be for the people, our people.

Of course, we would have to work on obtaining a liquor license and we all agreed that for the first few months, we would not offer food, just libations. It didn't make sense right from the get-go to jump into the restaurant business without testing the waters. We would concentrate on first establishing ourselves as a jazz club.

Our discussion also included the fact that Perseverance Hall would have to adhere to the laws of segregation and be a "colored-only" establishment. However, we agreed we would be willing to take the fallout of what would happen if the law came to our doors and saw there were blacks and whites together in the same room, having drinks and just enjoying the jazz. We were united in our thought process that although the law doesn't allow blacks and whites to commingle, we would.

Now that it was official that Johnny and Tee were agreeable to going into business with me on Perseverance Hall, I was eager to tell Gene. When we had our Sunday telephone call, I was bursting with excitement when I told him my news. It was important to me that he understood that my commitment to the club was not a permanent one. I explained to Gene that after a year of my self-gratifying experience, I intended to turn it over to Johnny and Tee.

But I first wanted to make sure they were set up and had a handle on the business. I figured a year was a good amount of time for them to get a grasp on managing the jazz club. Hopefully, it would be successful and they would want to continue with the venture. But if our expectations were not met, we would sell it.

After I finished telling Gene my thrilling news he said, "Pierre I am so happy for you! You deserve this opportunity and I am sure it will be a fantastic club. I can't wait to come and see it for myself." Gene's enthusiasm meant a great deal to me; he believed in me. I told Gene I was so appreciative of his support and I couldn't wait for him to get the grand tour of what I would be calling Perseverance Hall. The rest of our conversation was mostly about all of the work that needed to be done on the club before we could have our grand opening, which I was optimistic could happen in two months. Therefore, I asked him if he could wait a month before he purchased his ticket to come to NOLA. That way, I would have a better idea of the progress that had been made. Gene said, "Of course and I want to congratulate you on the name you have chosen. I can't think of a more appropriate name for your club. The word perseverance defines you and everything you have been through and continue to tackle and take on. You don't give up Pierre! With your persistence, I believe it is going to be a success!"

The following week, the deed was drawn up with Johnny, Tee and my name on it for Perseverance Hall. We worked with the bank and the attorneys to get the back taxes paid and all the financial matters taken care of. Mark was true to his word and the contractors met with us and we discussed our game plan. Within the week, the renovations started!

Gene and I continued talking on the telephone once a week. I was very much looking forward to his visit to NOLA over the summer. Things were really coming together with the work being done on the club. After a month, we were confident Perseverance Hall would be able to open within the two months I had hoped for.

Our grand opening was scheduled to take place in early summer of that year. It also would be a celebration of Gene's and my union but that information was not shared with anyone outside of my immediate circle of family and friends. Flordie insisted on catering the entire event. She would have her assistant Faith work with her. Faith was Mark's wife so it would be somewhat of a family affair on many levels. We worked out the menu which was going to be a simple one. Depending on what seafood was available at the time, we would have a seafood boil! In addition to the seafood, the pots would be filled with potatoes, corn, garlic and mushrooms. Flordie also said she would make loaves of crusty bread to accompany the meal along with a luscious grape cake! I told her I loved that idea. It would be our union grape cake!

Since everything was on track and falling into place, I was confident to set the date for our grand opening. I sent Gene a telegram with the date and asked if he could come a few days before the event and then stay a few days after. Much to my delight, I received a telegram back from Gene a few days later letting me know he and Michele had purchased their train tickets!

Johnny, Tee and I spent the next several weeks at Perseverance Hall getting it ready for our big day. Although it was labor intensive, we enjoyed every aspect of the work that needed to be done. It was our baby and we loved it dearly.

It felt like forever since I had last seen Gene and I was getting very excited to have him back in NOLA and in my arms. My wait was finally over when Gene and Michele arrived a few days before our opening. After leaving the train station, Greg dropped Gene and me off at Perseverance Hall. When we pulled up to the building, Gene ran up to the front door and asked if he could go in. It filled me with joy that he was so encouraging of this new part of my life and his excitement even brought me to a new level of enthusiasm. He dove right in and worked with the contractors helping to put the finishing touches on Perseverance Hall.

We stayed there for a few hours. But it was getting late, and I wanted to go home. I had other things on my mind. We had a light supper and some of the wine that he brought with him before turning in. This time when Gene pulled out a large bag of grapes, I wasn't surprised. He told me that he wanted to work with Flordie to make our grape union cake. I realized I was very fortunate to have a man who was so versatile. Not only was he good with his hands and doing manual labor, he knew his way around a kitchen and could bake our cake! Most importantly, he knew the way around my heart.

It was finally the afternoon of our grand opening/union party! I was so happy to see: Johnny, Tee, Maria, Greg, Michele, Flordie, Mark and Faith, my CC's – Irene, Dee, and Erina, Mary Grace and Michael, Rebecca and Walt, all the members of the Lagniappe Orchestra and even Richard from the Metairie Cemetery was there.

Just as I had envisioned when I contemplated purchasing Perseverance Hall, every table had low-light candles burning and small vases with pink roses in them. Everything I ever wanted in my life was there at Perseverance Hall that day. One of the greatest surprises was when Miss Loretta and Rooster entered and came over to me! They both gave me a hug and Rooster quickly touched my leg before anyone was the wiser.

The food, Jazz, Cajun music and the people were all

awesome. Like the seafood boil we served, our guests were a melting pot: blacks, whites, Catholics, Baptists, agnostics, police officers, criminals, former prostitutes, farmers, newspaper writers, business owners, singers, musicians, whiskey, wine and grape juice drinkers. Both the upstanding and down-right dirty citizens of NOLA all came out for our festivities! It was a rainbow of colors and backgrounds, all part of a collective group of people; my people.

Later that evening after all our guests had gone, Gene and I along with Johnny, Tee and Maria sat down to enjoy a final nightcap. I told Johnny and Tee that I would not be around Perseverance Hall that week as I wanted to be able to spend as much time with Gene as possible before he returned to Naples. They assured me they would have things under control since we hired quite a few new employees to work at Perseverance Hall. Even Maria was chipping in with the cleaning and any other chores her parents assigned to her. I told them they were doing a fantastic job taking care of all aspects of the management of the club. They in turn told me they were so appreciative to be able to have the opportunity to run our venture and still be able to perform right at our club if and when they wanted to do so. Life was good for all of us.

AMEN

Gene and I spent the few days after the grand opening catching up on our lives and being with each other from sun up to sun down. Since our long-distance relationship didn't allow for that daily, the time we did have together was so precious to both of us. We didn't want to make many plans for the week as we just wanted to go with the flow. Although, we did plan to meet Greg and Michele for dinner the night before Gene and Michele would be returning to Naples.

Whenever Gene left to go home, I was overcome with sadness. This time was no different. I didn't want him to go but I still wasn't at the point where I could go with him. Even though I was not in the best mood, there was no way I was going to put a damper on the night's dinner with Greg and Michele. Especially, since it would be the last time I would be sharing a meal with Gene until I visited him in Naples in the fall.

The four of us met at a quaint bistro a block away from St. Louis Cathedral. Before eating dinner, Greg ordered a bottle of champagne and proposed a toast. He said, "To good friends and new possibilities. We want you and Gene to know that Michele and I are engaged! The two of you have shown us that with love, all things are possible. We love each other deeply and want to start a family." The four of us all hugged each other and I told them I was so happy for them. Michele showed us her engagement ring. It was an exquisite marquise diamond with two baguette diamonds on the side. When I saw it, I couldn't help but say, "Greg, I believe you supersized the diamond! And Michele, I believe the man truly loves you and he has shown his commitment to you with the beautiful ring you are wearing on your finger."

Both of them were brimming with excitement for their upcoming nuptials. Michele explained that since she came from a large family, they would be getting married in Naples at the end of October, and her step-brother, Judge Higby would be officiant for the ceremony. Greg told us that his parents had passed away. He mentioned that his only living relative was his brother, Allen, who resides in New Orleans and would be attending the wedding in Naples. Michele also shared she would be moving to New Orleans and looked forward to finding a job in the newspaper industry. I winked at Greg and said, "I bet there is someone I know who will put in a good word for you."

That night after dinner, Gene and I went over to Jackson Square and sat on our favorite bench. He held my hand and asked me if I wanted to move out to the grape farm. However, as soon as he said that, he buffered the request with "Please know, Pierre, I wouldn't ask that of you until you were ready. So, I will not bring it up again but felt I needed to ask. I am a realistic man and know that may never be what you want to do. You have your newly found family and from what I have witnessed, a tremendous number of friends who love and support you. Also, I know you still want to perform with your band on special occasions and since you just purchased Perseverance Hall, you need to see where that takes you. I would never ask you to give that up. All I can say is I am still tied to the grape farm and can't give that up right now. We will just travel back and forth to each other's homesteads until we can no longer do that. I believe that circumstances and our feelings will guide our decisions going forward. But for now, I am just reeling in my newfound life with you, my wife."

That night, Gene held me throughout the entire night's sleep. It was like he couldn't bear to let me go. In the morning, we discussed the next time I would see him in Naples. We decided we would wait and see when Greg and Michele decided on a date for their October wedding and I would come back then. What I found was that as long as I had a plan to see Gene in the future, I could handle the sorrow of our leaving each other.

Greg and Michele picked us up in the morning to take us to the train station. I made the situation light for all of us by discussing their upcoming wedding. None of us wanted to talk about our heartaches. When we arrived, I held on to Gene for a brief moment and gently kissed his lips but didn't say the word, "goodbye." As had become our custom, we would then go our separate ways. Greg and Michele were also dealing with going their separate ways in their own fashion. On the ride home, Greg asked if I would like to have a drink. I told him I appreciated his offer, however, I needed time to be alone and asked him if he could drop me off around Jackson Square so I could go to the St. Louis Cathedral.

I was in a quandary over the situation Gene and I were going through. The question for both of us became, how do we each give up what is all comforting to oneself, everything we have ever known, and put ourselves out there for the unknown? There was no definitive answer and we didn't want to have the ultimate talk about how our lives would play out. And now with my purchasing Perseverance Hall, I wanted the opportunity to see if I could turn it into something I would be proud of. The same was true for Gene with his management of the grape farm. He wanted to see if he could turn it into a highly sought-after piece of property. In the interim, he wanted to have Walch's Grape Juice company continue to purchase the tonnage of grapes that the Wilcox farm could produce on an annual basis. We both were at exciting crossroads in our lives but still wanted to be with each other at the end of those roads. Neither of us knew what we could give up to make the life we wanted happen. We were resolute that we would forever be together, just unsure how much total togetherness we would ever be able to have. My identity was that I was a woman who lived in NOLA and loved that I did.

While sitting in St. Louis Cathedral, the most revered place of my life, I prayed. Guidance was what I was so in need of. As I replayed the past couple of years of my life, I found myself quietly expressing gratitude to God for all he had given me. "Most of all for my family, friends and Gene. The relationship I have with him has brought me a sense of security and happiness I never thought I would find. I know Gene is not a perfect man and I realize I am not a perfect woman. But we are perfect together. Where I am a perfectionist and can't let things go, Gene has a get-it-done mindset. He is reserved and quiet whereas I am a far cry from quiet. I have always lived my life out loud and proud. Staying in makes him happy whereas being out and about is what I like. He is analytical and I have been known to be illogical, not using the best reasoning. I see myself as patient and kind, while he can come across as hard and gruff with others, but gentle with me. I wear my heart on my sleeve and he keeps his tucked up tight in his farmer's overalls. But both of our hearts are in the right place and they belong to each other."

Noon Mass was starting so I put my thoughts aside to be mentally present for the service. However, I couldn't help but ask myself where I would be without Gene. The answer was although I had the love of my family and friends, I would still have had an empty heart. There was not a day that I regretted meeting him and having him in my life. I am not sure how our love story will play out but it definitely is a love story.

I found comfort in the Mass. It was when the priest gave his sermon about Jesus' first miracle which took place at a wedding in Cana, that I believed I found the sign I was looking for. With Jesus changing water into wine at that wedding, it demonstrated his power over all things. The sermon was to teach us that Jesus can provide for our needs and amazing things are possible when we have faith in him and follow his teachings. Also, with the sermon about wine, I felt it was a connection to my grape farmer. My faith was fortified that day and I believed things would work out for Gene and me. After Mass, on the way out of the church, I lit a candle and said to myself, "Dear God, I am placing my faith in you. All my life you have looked out for me and I am confident you will continue to do so. Amen – so be it."

NEW BEGINNINGS

The next few months were so rewarding for me. Perseverance Hall was doing very well. We hired an additional cleaner, bartender and maintenance man and we even started serving a limited food menu. Johnny and Tee would perform there usually on Wednesday and Friday evenings with the Lagniappe Orchestra and I would join them but just for a few songs. The rest of the acts were local bands that we knew of and we even had one night a week where new up-and-coming singers and musicians could showcase their abilities. We believe anyone who has worked hard to reach a certain level of performance deserves an opportunity, and we are happy to provide that.

The nice thing about having Perseverance Hall was that I didn't need to make a point of keeping in touch with all of my friends. Everyone important to me, would stop in and see me there. It was a place where we could all come together in music and friendship and of course libations!

Even though I was so busy with everything I had

going on in my life, I still missed Gene. Greg, his brother Allen, and I would be leaving in a couple of weeks to go to Naples for Greg and Michele's wedding. I was so looking forward to seeing Gene and I was very excited to be part of Greg and Michele's wedding. They had asked me if I would sing "Lace Around the Moon" at their ceremony and I was honored.

The night before leaving for our trip, there was a little get-together at Perseverance Hall for Greg. It was a bachelor party of sorts but on a scaled-down level without any improprieties. Johnny and Tee told me they had a surprise for me; there would be a new, up-and-coming singer performing that night who they believed I would love to hear.

When I arrived, every table had a low-light candle on it. I sat down at my favorite table where a whiskey – neat, was waiting for me. I have to admit I was intrigued to see who this new performer was that they had so been excited for me to see. Johnny and the band were all set and ready to go. Tee came to the stage area and asked for everyone to give a warm welcome to a local young lady who would be singing a song that was very meaningful to her. It took my breath away when Maria came onto the stage and sang, "Lace Around the Moon." I sat there spellbound and I heard patrons say, "Pierre, go up there and join her." I shook my head and said, "No, this is Maria's moment to shine." She performed a few other songs and when she was done, she walked over to my table, bent down and kissed me. The crowd erupted in applause and I erupted in tears. It was then I realized, my granddaughter would be following in my footsteps as a singer on some level. After her performance, I believe she would be sought after to perform around NOLA.

Many years ago, when I first performed at TCA's pleasure club, I got a taste of how it felt to perform for others and be respected and admired for my singing voice. The same thing happened to Maria that night. There is no other feeling like it and you can't help but want that euphoric state to continue. The most wonderful thing for me was when I heard her sing like that, I heard my voice coming through hers as they sounded similar. However, her vocal range was stronger and more beautiful than mine; I couldn't have been any prouder of my girl!

The following morning, Greg, Allen and I headed to Naples. The train ride was a joyous one and we were able to really talk with each other. I felt like I got to know more about Greg than I ever had. He and Allen told me all about their childhood and their family. Greg was an amazing man and I felt so blessed to have him as my friend and have him in my life. I truly thought of him as my second son.

When we arrived at the station, Gene and Michele

were there to greet us. I looked at Gene and my heart just kept fluttering. His arms were open to me and I ran into them. I was craving his loving enfold. He lifted my chin and his lips found mine. It was a long, much-needed kiss for both of us. We quickly said goodbye to Greg, Allen and Michele. I just wanted to get back to the grape farm with my farmer.

Two days later, Gene and I went to the Naples Hotel for Greg and Michele's wedding and reception. It was an elegant affair on all levels. One of the things I loved regarding the ceremony was that her step-brother, Judge Higby performed the service with the two of them exchanging their vows on a beautiful settee that was used at the Naples Hotel. It truly was a loveseat on which Greg and Michele professed their love for each other and their commitment to their marriage. The festivities lasted for several hours which included a delicious meal and dancing. The night ended with me singing "Lace Around the Moon" a cappella. It was the most heartfelt gift I could think of to give to my dear friend Greg and his beautiful new wife.

As I sat there next to Gene, watching Greg and Michele have their first dance together as man and wife, I was so happy for them. And I was happy for myself. As I looked around the Naples Hotel, I thought of all the times I spent there over the past couple of years and realized it was one of the places I had come to love, along with St. Louis Cathedral, Jackson Square, Perseverance Hall and the grape farm. So many monumental, life-changing events happened at those places and they all felt like home to me.

NEUTRAL GROUNDS

Neutral ground is what we New Orleanians call meridians, the little strip of ground in the middle of the road. Legend has it that neutral ground got its name from the early French and the Spanish who could do business between sections of the city standing on the neutral ground. As Gene and I continued to age, our traveling between our two cities would one day no longer be possible. We were both looking for a place that could be our neutral ground.

We eventually made a plan for our future. Gene would come to visit me in New Orleans in July. I would then go back to the grape farm in October as I needed the reassuring smell of the grapes and the warmth of his hands when he would hold mine as we walked through the vineyard together. Gene, in turn, would come to NOLA for two weeks around the holidays. To fill the time in between, we continued our letter-writing and telephone calls. Then every April, on our anniversary, I would take a train to Buffalo. Gene would pick me up and we would go stay at the Shamrock Inn for a week and just be Gene and Pierre in our Gene-Pierre world. Not a jazz singer and club owner from New Orleans or a farm manager from Naples, just two people who found love and wanted to spend time together on neutral ground. After the week in Buffalo, I would spend an additional three weeks at the grape farm.

Gene and I knew we would need to meet in the middle of many aspects of our lives. Neither of us could give up our identities, nor had we expected the other to do so. The way we saw it was, *laissez les bon temps rouler* – let the good times roll! And when we could no longer roll alone, we would decide where we would roll together.

I never told Gene that I looked into the possibility of purchasing a small blueberry farm in Covington, Louisiana. The location was about an hour outside of NOLA. Since I knew how important tending to the fields and having his hands in the soil was to him, I thought that might be appealing. Also, at some point, he might decide the harsh and cold winters in Naples were just too hard on maturing bones and he would welcome NOLA's warmth. However, unless he comes to these conclusions on his own without my enticement, that conversation will not be had. But truth be told, I hope we do someday have that conversation.

TO STOP AND SENSE THE GRAPES

We continued to live our lifestyle and it worked for us. Every time I would visit Gene at the grape farm, we had a wonderful time. Even if we hadn't seen each other in a couple of months, we always picked up where we left off, without skipping a beat.

One evening after we finished dancing in the living room at the grape farm, I told Gene I had a gift for him, a gift that came from my heart. With each of us having a glass of his wine in our hands, I read him a poem I wrote for him…

TO STOP AND SENSE THE GRAPES

Letting go of all I held onto wasn't easy to do.
But with my having your secure love, things changed because
of you.
It was different to live in the moment and seize the day
And for the first time having the attitude of come what may.
Spending time with you has heightened all of my senses
And also helped me break through some of my defenses
To Stop and Sense the Grapes.

Seeing the grapes so full hanging down low on the rows of
vines
Brings back heartfelt thoughts of the times we shared your
delicious wine.
My **eyes** focus in on the beauty of the clusters
As they bask in the sunlight enhancing their luster.

Hearing the grapes pop as I bite into their delicate skin
Stirs up intense feelings that I have which come from deep
within.
My **ears** take in all of the vineyard's audible sounds
That come from nature that is abundantly around.

Tasting the grapes that you and I picked together in the fall
Is a memory I hold dear and will forever recall.
My **tongue** is enticed by the delectable flavors
Whether dry or sweet, both of which I long to savor.

Touching the grapes that are white, rose or red is a pleasure
That will stay in my mind and that I will forever treasure.
My **hands** grasp the bunches that look like amethyst gems
As they are cascading down from their connected stems.

Smelling the grapes' fragrance as it wafts up into the crisp air
Is a delightful memory I am grateful we could share.
My **nose** breathes in aromas during harvesting days.
As I marvel at the stunning landscape on display.

Somehow, I always found the will and the strength to persevere.
Your steadfast embrace helped me overcome most of my fears.
With your secure love, I have now become unfrozen and free.
So many aspects of my life coming full circle for me.
My closed doors have all opened and so have my senses.
I now live out loud and not under false pretenses

To Stop and Sense the Grapes

After I finished, he simply held me tight and said "Pierre, you said that the poem is a gift for me and I absolutely love it! However, the greatest gift in my life has been spending time with you." I looked into his beautiful blue eyes and tears of joy spilled out of mine as I replied, "Gene, you taught me how to stop and smell the grapes and the secure love you have given me is one of the most precious gifts I have ever been blessed to receive."

As I said before, words are so powerful; especially written words. Not only did I give Gene my secure love with the poem, I also gave him my words.

EPILOGUE

I am not saying my story has ended. I am just saying I no longer feel the need to tell it. Looking back on all of the aspects of my life, I always tried to do for others. To me, that mattered a great deal and with that belief and practice, my life was complete. When it comes time for me to leave this earth, I will be able to pass on with no regrets. It took my lifetime of making amends to get to that point but I did.

And if more of my story should still be told, I hope it is my granddaughter Maria, who finishes telling it for me. Or perhaps she will have her own story to tell. I decided a while ago to let sleeping dogs lie with regard to who her grandfather might have been. But with her inquisitive mind and appetite for many things in life, I believe she will one day look into exactly who her people were on her mama's side and what a story that could be. After all, things are passed down in a family and family is above all, but you must first know who they are.

ABOUT THE AUTHOR

Mary Pierre Quinn-Stanbro is from Buffalo, NY and currently resides there. She is married to Gene Stanbro and plans to eventually move to the Gene-Pierre Vineyard in Naples, NY. She is retired from the Federal Government after providing 34 years of public service. Mary Pierre is working on having *The Berry-Picker House, Lace Around the Moon* and *The Grape Farm* (trilogy) possibly turned into a television series, play or movie.

Mary Pierre also co-authored *The Bond of Blue* with Michele Graves, which was published in 2021. It is a tribute to her father, Francis Quinn and her grandfather Frank Quinn. They were both Buffalo Police Officers. The book showcases their time with the Buffalo Police Department and shares stories of actual cases her grandfather was involved with during his time with the Department, including a still open cold case.

The story is dedicated to her family members who served or are currently serving in law enforcement and to all members of law enforcement, especially the Buffalo Police Department.

Mary Pierre has an Associate's Degree from Trocaire College and a Bachelor's Degree from Buffalo State College. She has always wanted to share her writing with others and is blessed to still be doing so.